HE CLAIMS ME

Also by Cynthia Sax

He Touches Me
He Watches Me

HE
CLAIMS ME

The Seen Trilogy: Part Three

CYNTHIA SAX

An Imprint of HarperCollinsPublishers

CLAIMS ME

This is a work of fiction. Names, characters, places, and incidents are products of the author's imagination or are used fictitiously and are not to be construed as real. Any resemblance to actual events, locales, organizations, or persons, living or dead, is entirely coincidental.

EPub Edition JULY 2013 ISBN: 9780062300348
Print Edition ISBN: 9780062300355

10 9 8 7 6 5 4 3 2

For my dear wonderful hubby
for proving that true love exists.
And also for Tessa Woodward, my fabulous editor,
for believing in The Seen Trilogy and in me.
You've made me a better writer and I truly appreciate it!

HE CLAIMS ME

Chapter One

I CAN CONTROL my desires and do my job. I can. I sort through the manila files, the box containing them bound for storage. I won't think about Blaine Technologies' enigmatic CEO, my boss's boss.

Is Blaine thinking of me? Is he remembering how earlier tonight I kneeled in front of him, both of us positioned before his office's floor-to-ceiling windows? He'd been gloriously naked, all muscle, tanned skin, and silver scars, his cock hard and his hips thrust forward as I sucked him, taking him deep inside my mouth, his salty essence coating my tongue.

Anyone standing on the sidewalk below could have seen me worshipping Gabriel Blaine's body, showing the billionaire CEO and my temporary neighbor how much I trusted him. I allowed him to use me for his selfish pleasure and I loved it.

I want him to use me again. I wiggle in place as I place

the files in alphabetical order. There's no one to see me dance. It's almost midnight and the floor is deserted, the fluorescent lights dimmed, the space quiet except for the hum of a faraway printer.

Sweat trickles down my neck and my shoulders ache. Although I'm tired, every cell in my body is aware that Blaine is physically near, sequestered behind the closed office door to my right, working as hard as I am. He runs his technology empire. I rearrange his files.

We're alone. Fran, my boss and Blaine's assistant, has left for the evening. An envelope marked with my name is propped against a box on my desk. It contains my pay for the night, an astronomical sum for an evening of easy work. I flip through the files faster, determined to earn the salary, to not disappoint her or Blaine, to be worthy.

"It's time to go home, Anna," a deep sexy voice rumbles.

I jump, my heart pounding. Blaine stands with his arms folded and his legs braced apart, watching me, always watching me. He's dressed once more in his black suit, white shirt, his tie tightly knotted under his angular face. His green eyes glitter, the lights reflecting off his black hair.

I suck in my breath, my body humming to life. Blaine isn't classically handsome but he's striking and, in this moment, he's mine. I want him more than I've ever wanted anyone, my pussy moistening and my nipples tightening.

I close the box I'm working on and slip the envelope of cash into my black faux leather tote. "You pay me too much for this job." I clasp the tote tightly as we walk to the bank of elevators, my flat black shoes making no sound on the plush gray carpet.

Blaine shrugs his broad shoulders. "Fran decided upon your wages." He presses the button and doors open immediately as though the elevator has been waiting for us. I enter the mirrored car first and Blaine follows, pushing P1 for the parking garage.

He stands close to me, too close for a simple CEO-employee relationship. The sandalwood and musk of his cologne teases my nostrils. His body heat encircles me, warming me all over.

Blaine is powerful, a man in his prime, at the top of his game, and a tremor of excitement rolls over me. He has promised to take me in the elevator. Is tonight the night? I stroke the silver railing back and forth, back and forth, the metal cool under my fingers, and I picture clearly how I'll please him.

I'll suck his cock first, easing some of his desire, allowing him to regain control, to resist taking me completely, my billionaire CEO respecting my boundaries more than I do. I'm a virgin, having never trusted a man enough to let him inside me. I peek up at Blaine's stern face. I might, maybe tonight, maybe tomorrow, maybe never, trust him enough.

But now, at this moment, I'll drop to my knees before him and unzip his pants. Blaine will watch me, his emotions concealed behind the blank mask he wears with others, his hands clenched behind his back. He won't touch me, he doesn't dare, fearing loss of his renowned control. He'll allow me to service him and I *will* service him, with passion, with caring.

His crisp white cotton boxer shorts and black pants will drop to his ankles, revealing his hard cock. I lick my lips, the taste of him lingering in my mouth. I'll close my fingers around his base, holding him as I rub my lips over his smooth tip. A bead of pre-cum will form on his slit and I'll lave him with the flat of my tongue. I'll see, via the mirror, his ass cheeks clench, his ironclad restraint tested by my touch.

"Not here," Blaine rumbles, shaking me from my reverie.

I glance up at him, not surprised he's read my naughty thoughts. He has always been able to read me, to see me. He is the only person who ever has.

Blaine's eyes are dark and his body is coiled, lowered, as though readying to pounce, heavy waves of warmth rolling off his muscular physique. A connection pulses between us, an awareness, both sexual and spiritual.

"And not now?" My voice is husky. I lick my lips again.

His gaze tracks the movement. "Not now," Blaine agrees, leaning into me. I submit to him, tilting my head back, my frizzy hair cascading down my back, the tendrils sweeping my suit-covered ass. We remain locked in this position, his dominance exciting me.

The elevator bell rings and the doors open, cooler air blasting us back to reality. Blaine exits first, holding the elevator doors open for me. His sleek black limousine idles nearby.

"Mr. Blaine. Miss Sampson." Ted, his driver, opens

the back door. He's clad in a black suit, white shirt, black skinny tie, black cap, and there's a knowing glint in his brown eyes.

Blaine and I have used the limousine for encounters before and Ted has watched us. Yesterday, he saw me completely naked, heard me cry out with fulfillment as Blaine ravished my pussy with his rough, coarse fingers. I shiver, my sexual needs escalating.

"Did you pick up the suits from Fran?" Blaine pauses before the luxurious vehicle. He flattens one of his hands on the small of my back, his touch possessive and reassuring, his ownership of my body clear.

"Yes, sir." Ted bobs his head, his expression as blank as his boss's. "They're in the backseat as you instructed, Mr. Blaine."

I climb into the vehicle, breathing in the interior's new car smell, and I claim the seat facing the driver, placing my tote on the black carpet. A garment bag hangs against the heavily tinted windows. A mysterious black shopping bag rests against the interior wall.

Blaine sits across from me, stretching his long legs out. The door closes and the lights slightly dim. There's a jolt followed by a vibration under my ass. We're moving.

Blaine watches me, his gaze as soft and as heated as a caress, and I watch him. He appears ruthlessly hard, honed from stone, but I know he can be hurt. He's shown me the scars on his body, the vulnerability in his soul.

He flips his hands over, revealing his lined palms. "Here, Anna." Blaine's eyes gleam, the angles in his face growing more pronounced.

He'll touch me here in the limousine. My toes curl inside my black flat-heeled shoes. I slowly unbutton my navy blue and lavender stripe blazer, one piece of the vintage Chanel suit Fran, my boss, has given me.

Rolling my shoulders, I teasingly lower the garment, revealing my pale skin, reveling in the power I have over the men, both men. I'm not only stripping for Blaine. The partition between the driver and us is lowered. Ted also watches me.

Will Blaine allow him to do more than watch tonight? I hesitate, my fingers fluttering over my blazer's lion buttons, doubts dousing my desire. I don't want another man touching me. I only feel safe and beautiful and cherished with Blaine.

"I chose here because having an audience excites you." Blaine tilts his head toward the lowered partition. "It excites me also but I won't put you at risk, not now, not ever. I'll control who watches us, where they watch, and what they watch. No one will ever touch or hurt you."

"Thank you." My desire flares once more, rekindled by his vow, a vow I know he'll keep. I drop the blazer onto the seat and cool air grazes over my collarbone.

Blaine is right. Having an audience excites me. I pull my black tank top over my head, mussing my hair and revealing my pretty white bra, the shell-shaped cups barely concealing my small breasts.

What will Ted watch tonight? I skim my fingers over the delicate cotton. Will Blaine take my virginity? I pinch my nipples through the fabric, the sharp pain thrilling me. Am I ready for this step, to have him completely inside me, to trust him this much?

I run my hands over my bra, squeezing and lifting, toying with my two men and with myself. Blaine shifts in his seat, his dress pants tented around an impressively large erection. He wants to be inside me and I *do* trust him, more than I trust anyone, more than I trust myself.

I wiggle out of my a-line skirt. Is this level of trust enough? I brush my fingers over the soft cotton panties, caressing, teasing myself. The fabric is wet, slicked with my juices. Can I do this?

"Show me everything, nymph," Blaine orders.

I unhook my bra, freeing my breasts, my nipples taut. The gold key giving me access to Blaine's backyard dangles between my breasts, its black ribbon looping around my neck.

Blaine gazes at me, his eyes glowing with an admiration I now believe in. He loves my body, my slight curves, the full triangle of closely cropped brown curls over my mons.

I pull my panties down and spread my legs, shamelessly allowing him to look at me, all of me. My pink pussy lips glisten with moisture. Ted is looking at me also, perusing skin he'll never touch.

"Beautiful." Blaine sinks to his knees before me, humbling himself, and I tremble, tilting my ass up, opening wider for him. He brushes his scarred knuckles over my knees and up my inner thighs, his caress gentle, almost reverent.

"You're wet for me." His grim lips curl into a smug smile.

"I'm always wet for you." I place my palms over my breasts, gripping them and releasing, fondling myself into a frenzy. "Only for you."

Blaine strokes my pussy up and down, up and down, drawing more moisture from my core, more tremors from my body. I pinch my nipples to his rhythm, edging the pleasure with pain.

He leans forward, his dark head positioned between my pale thighs, his hard angles wedged between my soft curves, our visual contrasts stimulating me. "You smell delicious." His hot breath wafts on my skin, his mouth close, so close to that aching part of me. "How do you taste?"

My breath hitches and I still, the tension in my body snapping tight. Blaine meets my gaze and holds it as he extends his tongue, drawing nearer, nearer, nearer, moving slowly, too slowly. I need him—

He taps my clit with his tongue and I cry out, lifting my hips. Desire surges along my legs, courses up my chest, heating every inch of me.

"Easy." Blaine cups my ass, restraining, controlling, my wiggling body, his rough touch exciting me. My form is no longer my own. My responses belong to him.

I squirm, lifting my gaze over his shoulder, seeing the driver's brown hair through the partition. In my fantasy he's watching me through the rearview mirror, wanting me, his cock hard.

Blaine licks me from ass to clit with his flat, hot, wet tongue, and my fantasy dissipates, replaced by an even more exquisite reality. "Delicious." He smacks his lips, his green eyes glowing with a heartwarming sincerity, and I quiver in his hands.

"Please." I ask him for more, not knowing what this more is, having progressed past my limited realm of experience.

Blaine lowers his head and mouths over my folds, rubbing his nose against my clit. I squirm and writhe as he licks and laves my sensitive flesh. A rumble of appreciation rolls up his chest as he eats me out with a gratifying gusto, as though he's never tasted anything as delectable as my pussy.

I thread my fingers through his black hair, freeing his rebellious locks. The strands fall over his forehead and I tighten my hold on his beloved scalp, Blaine being my constant in this unreliable world. With him, I don't have to worry about being judged, being found wanting. He knows my father died in prison and my mother abandoned me, and he sees strength in my survival. He loves my body and laughs at my antics. He thinks I'm delicious.

Blaine kisses and nips my pussy, his love bites varying from soothing and light to fierce and sharp, keeping me thrillingly off balance. I moan, swishing my ass, unable to keep still.

He growls, his lips humming against my folds, and he grips me tighter, his animalistic sounds exhilarating. I am woman. I am powerful and his, having the ability to strain his control.

Blaine probes my entrance with his tongue, sliding his flesh along mine, and I arch, the experience unlike any I've ever known. I've filled my pussy with my fingers, his fingers, a hard marble dildo, but never a tongue and never Blaine's tongue. He thrusts deeper and deeper inside me, pressing his nose against my clit, pushing his chin against me.

"Yes, Blaine. Yes." I pump my hips, pulling him into me, beating my pussy against his lips, and he kneads my ass, coaxing me faster, harder, wilder. My juices smatter his tanned cheeks as I slap and grind against his face.

Blaine strokes inside me, flicks my clit, strokes and flicks, strokes and flicks. Tremors rock my body. My ass cheeks shake in his big palms. I dig my short, blunt fingernails into his scalp, branding him as he brands me.

He ravishes my pussy, strumming me with his tongue, his renowned focus fixed on me and only me. It is a heady feeling, more intoxicating than the strongest alcohol.

"Blaine?" I'm close, so close, primed by my fantasies and the endless waiting, wanting, needing.

"Come for me, Anna." His lips vibrate against my folds, his words felt in my soul. "Come for me. Now." Blaine fixes his hot mouth over my clit and sucks.

I scream, driving upward, my ass leaving the leather seat, and my darkness bursts into vivid color as I plunge head first into a pool of pleasure, waves of warmth, of satisfaction washing over me. I cling to Blaine and he clasps me as securely, his lips on my pussy and his fingers under me.

I float, euphoric, my body limp and my limbs heavy. Blaine licks and sucks, draining the moisture from my pussy, cleaning me carefully, thoroughly.

"That was wonderful." I repeat the first words I've ever said to him.

"I agree." Blaine brushes his lips against mine and I taste myself. "That *was* wonderful, natural and real."

He remembers his reply to me. I blink back tears, a warmth spreading over my chest. Before meeting Blaine, I was invisible, but he sees me. He listens to me. He remembers.

"*This* is real." He grips my nape and leans his forehead against mine. The tips of our noses touch, and his breath rushes over my lips. Specks of moisture glisten on his tanned skin. I slide my hands between his jacket and his cotton shirt. I'm naked and he's fully dressed.

I swivel my hips. He's also hard, the ridge in his dress pants large and unyielding. I push against him.

Blaine groans and pulls away, returning to the seat across from me. My legs are parted, my body bare and exposed. I glance at the partition. The driver continues to look straight ahead. He must have heard me scream, must have watched me as I came. Did he come too? Are his pants splattered with his essence? Another tremor rolls over me, a poignant echo of the pleasure I've experienced.

"How do you feel, nymph?" Blaine asks, his eyelids partially lowered, a small smile curling his lips.

"Cherished." I smile back at him. "And I wish for you to feel the same way." I lower my gaze to his groin. His black dress pants are pulled tightly over his unabated erection. "Tell me what you need." He satisfied me and I will now satisfy him.

Chapter Two

BLAINE UNFASTENS HIS pants and pulls the fabric down to his ankles, removing his stark white boxer shorts at the same time. He spreads his thighs and waits, allowing me to look at him as he earlier looked at me.

As I gaze at him, needs, yearnings, desires I thought fully sated resurface. Blaine is much larger than even the marble dildo we've used in the past, his cock jutting upward, long and thick and rigid. Short black curls cover his base, his balls hugging his shaft.

I want him inside me. A warm flush sweeps up my body. But I'm scared, scared I'll show him everything and he'll abandon me as everyone else has, taking that piece of me with him.

"Straddle me, nymph," Blaine orders, his curt tone demanding my full attention.

"Do you want me to suck you first?" I lick my bottom lip, nervous, my fears mounting.

"I'll always want you to suck me." Blaine's voice deepens.

Moisture drips down my inner thighs, my body reacting to his words. I continue to hesitate, torn between my lust for him and fear of the unknown.

"But I've already come once this evening," he states. "I can control myself if you straddle me." He wraps his fingers around his base as though offering his cock to me.

I won't turn down his offer. I slide onto his lap, trusting him to control himself. There's no reason not to trust him, as Blaine has never broken his word to me. His thighs flex under me, his power barely contained. He reaches back, presses a button, and the seat partially reclines.

"That's a clever feature." I pull his shirt higher, exposing more tanned skin and more silver scars, his violent past written upon his body.

"During long trips, I sometimes sleep here." Blaine's gaze intensifies. "Alone." He brushes my hair back from my flushed face, his touch gentle. "Always alone." He curls a brown lock around his index finger.

I flatten my palms over his lapels, splaying my fingers over his chest, understanding more than he's said. Before meeting Blaine, I was also a solitary creature, unheard and unseen, distrustful of everyone and everything.

"You're no longer alone, Blaine." I push my body forward, pressing my pussy lips against his shaft, tightening the bond between us.

"Yes, I'm no longer alone." He drops his hands to my hips. "I know what this is for us, Anna, but I'll wait for you." Blaine swirls his thumbs into my skin. "I won't rush and risk hurting you. I'll never hurt you."

"I know you'll never hurt me." He wouldn't intentionally hurt me but he thinks I'm strong and I'm not. I rock against him, slicking his cock with my juices. "What is this for us?" I brace emotionally for the answer. Is this an affair? A fling? A test of how long he can last without sex?

Blaine buries his face in the curve where my neck meets my shoulder, his warm breath wafting over my skin. "This is forever," he murmurs against my skin.

Forever. A tight band of emotion wraps around my chest, pressing down on my lungs, making it difficult to breathe. He'll never abandon me, never leave me. It's too much to hope for, to believe in. "Blaine?"

"Pleasure yourself with my body, Anna." Blaine redirects the conversation. Part of me is relieved, needing time to think about this new development, while another part of me is disappointed, yearning for verification.

"Tell me what you need and that's what I'll do." He outlines the rules to this new game. "That's all I'll do."

I'll be in control. I undulate against him, moving faster and faster, excited by his offer. We'll only go as far as I allow us. "I need your mouth on my neck." I tilt my head to the side, swinging my hair over my back.

Blaine drags his lips up and down my neck, his fervent caress stimulating my skin, his obedience moistening my pussy. His body is mine to use, mine to direct. I rub my feminine folds over his cock, my nipples over his suit jacket, the friction adding to the heady feeling of power.

He grazes my sensitive skin with his teeth, sending

waves of sensation down my form, and I moan, swiveling my hips, grinding into his shaft, shamelessly using him for my own satisfaction. I grip his nape, his hair soft against my fingertips.

Blaine bends his dark head and sucks on the base of my neck, his suction glorious and arousing. I rise up on him, a keening sound ripped from my lips. He releases my neck and I allow myself to fall, our bodies colliding. The gold key between my breasts bounces.

"Cup my ass." I grip Blaine's broad shoulders and pull myself up once more, climbing his hard physique. His big palms slide under me, supporting my weight. "That's it. I want to ride you."

He lifts me, stroking my pussy along his shaft, my clit along his rim, and he drops me, smacking my ass on his thighs. He lifts and drops, lifts and drops. I pant, my skin heating, and Blaine grunts, mouthing my neck, the sounds of our encounter filling the vehicle.

I roll my hips and he shudders, his controlled tempo thrown off by my action. I like throwing off his tempo, stressing his control, so I do it again. He hardens even more against me, a bead of pre-cum forming on his tip.

"Anna," he growls.

"I'm pleasuring myself with your body, Blaine." I flick his earlobe with my tongue, savoring the salt of his skin. "Your hard, hot body." Blaine's legs shake under me and the cords on his neck lift. I trace these cords with my lips, my tasting pulling a strangled noise from his throat.

"Faster," I order, seeking to break him, this powerful man. "Harder." I gasp as he obeys, driving me down on his thighs, his ass remaining motionless in the seat. "Lift into me."

"Yes." Blaine thrusts upward as I fall upon him. My ass and pussy throbs, his erotic abuse ratcheting my passion upward. As our bodies crash together, he nips my neck, marking me.

"Yes." I agree, my lungs and breasts aching. "Make my tight little pussy feel you for days." I grind into every slide. Sweat drips down my spine, between my ass cheeks, and a red flush covers Blaine's face. We work as one, reaching for our satisfaction, together.

I want him inside me, filling me, but I'm not ready, not yet. This is enough, the fucking without entry, the delicious slide of my curves against his hard muscles. My body tightens, the tension stretching unbearably thin, and I dangle on the edge, needing one more push.

"When I come, you come," I instruct. Blaine's fingers dig into my tender ass, his massive form shaking. I grit my teeth, holding off for as long as I can, not wanting this encounter to end, not wanting to leave him.

Tears stream down my face. I can't last. I can't. "Bite me, Blaine." I ask for the pain I need.

He closes his teeth over my shoulder, his teeth sharp, dangerous, right, and the tightness inside me breaks, snapping in two. I fling my arms back and cry his name, flying high on the winds of desire.

"Anna," Blaine roars, wrapping his arms around my waist, holding me to him. He drives his hips upward and hot cum splashes over my stomach, soothing the burn.

He thrusts two more times, shuddering, and he sags, burying his face between my small breasts, his forehead resting on the gold key.

I return to earth, trembling with exhaustion, and cradle his head in my hands, his black hair sinfully soft and decadently thick like the plush carpeting he has in his office.

Blaine leans backward, taking me with him. I rest my cheek on his silk tie and he props his chin on the top of my head. He strokes my bare back, drifting his fingertips over my spine, his touch soothing and right.

This isn't normal, I know, almost fucking in a limousine while the driver listens and watches. I don't care. Drowsy and sated, I snuggle deeper into Blaine's warm form.

He chuckles, hugging me closer. "You'll sleep more comfortably in a bed, nymph."

In a bed, not necessarily my bed. I raise my head and meet his gaze, my body stiffening. I'm not ready for this either. It's too soon, too much.

Blaine's eyes glint with unspoken promises. "Not tonight." He presses his lips to my forehead, his mouth hot. "Dress and I'll walk you to the Leighs' door."

At some time during the encounter we'd arrived home. We were parked in our upper class community while I screamed with satisfaction, our neighbors sleeping peacefully in the mansions around us. I look at the partition. Ted, our driver, remains behind the wheel, silently waiting for us to finish.

I retreat to my seat and dress quickly, not bothering to clean my skin with tissues, wanting Blaine's scent on me. He pulls his pants up, the tail of his white cotton shirt yellowed with his cum. I brush back my hair, trying to tame it, the tendrils frizzy.

"You look beautiful," Blaine assures me, admiration in his green eyes. I feel beautiful and cherished. Is it truly possible to feel this way forever? Can Blaine be right about our relationship lasting?

He hands me the mysterious black shopping bag. "Everything in here is for you," he states, knowing I'll never touch anything that isn't mine.

I peek inside, glimpsing a much-needed bottle of conditioner and a black velvet bag containing my favorite sex toy. "You're giving me the dildo." I frown, my excitement dissipating. Is he taking another business trip?

"That's for tonight." Red streaks across my billionaire's cheekbones. "I want you to sleep with it inside you."

"Oh." He's not leaving. I wiggle, giddy with relief. "You want me to use the dildo."

"Not use." Blaine's lips twitch. "Slide the dildo into your pussy. That's all. You're not to touch yourself or find release without me." He knocks on the window and the door opens.

Ted stands by the vehicle. The driver's spine is straight and his expression is carefully blank but he doesn't fool me. I know he watched our sex play, listened to my screams.

Blaine exits the limousine first, the garment bags draped over one of his shoulders, and he holds out his hand. I grasp his fingers with one hand, clutching the bag and my tote with the other.

On previous nights, Blaine released my hand once I was upright. Tonight he links our fingers together and walks with me, shortening his stride to match mine. My good mood bubbles over, my joy impossible to contain.

"It's like we're a couple," I muse. A normal couple.

"We *are* a couple." Blaine frowns and I blink, unaware I said the words out loud. "There's no one else for me, Anna. There hasn't been since the first moment I saw you."

"Oh." I tilt my head back and gaze up at the sky. The stars twinkle. The crescent moon hangs low. Are horny purple aliens watching us, waiting for us to strip naked, to touch ourselves? "There's been no one else since I first swam in your pool?"

"There's been no one else since you interviewed to house-sit for the Leighs." Blaine gazes upward also, his jaw jutted, his profile rugged and undeniably masculine. "And a little brown moth landed on your wrist."

"I remember." I kicked over the fallen leaf the moth was hiding under, startling the tiny creature. She flew upward, her wings fluttering, and she gripped me with her little legs, her entire body quivering. She looked as scared as I was, the prospect of meeting the Leighs terrifying me.

"You set the moth carefully on a rosebush, concealing her beneath the pink blooms." Blaine meets my gaze, his eyes soft, as though he treasures this simple memory.

"The gardener then yelled at me for walking on the

grass," I add ruefully. "He chased me halfway down the block, waving his hands and cursing at me." I shake my head, my cheeks heating. "Why would you have grass if you can't walk on it?" I ask, and Blaine gives me one of his rare smiles.

Silence stretches, a companionable quiet, and I walk even slower, in no rush to return to the Leighs' empty bungalow. "You saw the moth incident, huh?" I glance up at him. I was wearing my baggy white shirt and oversized black pants, thinking myself invisible, and he saw me.

"I watched you even then." Blaine squeezes my hand. "You were beautiful and real and I couldn't look away." He waits as I find my key, his gaze fixed on my face.

I feel cherished . . . maybe even loved, not that I remember what being loved feels like. The last person to love me was my father, and he died in prison when I was fourteen.

As Blaine and I stand on the Leighs' cold steel welcome mat, I fiddle with the finicky lock. Finally there's a click and the door swings open. Warm air rushes out of the concrete and glass modern bungalow, the air-conditioning too costly to run.

My agreement with Dr. Leigh and his wife is I pay for utilities and maintenance as they gallivant around Europe. In exchange, I get a place to stay.

Unfortunately, to pay for this deal I have to work two jobs. I work days at Feed Your Hungry, dialing for dollars at the charity, and I work nights at Blaine Technologies as an assistant to Fran, Blaine's assistant.

A wonderful upside of my second job is I spend more

time with Blaine. I smile at the Leighs' sexy neighbor, wishing I could invite him inside. I can't. The plastic surgeon and his wife left me with a long list of things I couldn't do while staying in their house, having visitors being top on this list.

Blaine hands me the garment bags. Our fingers brush and a spark of awareness shoots up my arm. "These are more suits from Fran," he explains.

"She wanted to throw the suits away." I raise my chin. Although there's no judgment in Blaine's deep voice, years of facing accusations have made me defensive. "She told me I could have them." I'm not a thief like my father. I don't take what isn't mine.

"Fran's happy you'll wear them." Blaine leans forward and glides his lips over mine, evaporating my concerns with one heated touch. "Remember my instructions for tonight." He taps the tip of my nose and I blink. "Be a good girl, Anna."

Blaine turns and walks away, his shoulders broad, his spine rigidly straight and proud. I close the door, flick on the hallway lights, and slip out of my shoes, as no shoes are allowed in the house.

I pad across the concrete floors, turning a light off for every light I turn on. I rearrange the selection of store catalogues on a modern glass hallway table and nudge a couple of Mrs. Leigh's geometric glass objets d'art an inch to the left, my goal to make the empty house appear lived in.

The door of a display case in the dining room has swung open. Touching Mrs. Leigh's display cases is another item on my not to do list, the brightly colored cones housed within them being the most valuable of her collection. Forced to break this rule, I carefully close the glass door using two of my fingers. Mrs. Leigh would become more upset if dust touched her precious knickknacks.

As I move through the house, sweat beads on my forehead, the heat stifling. I open some of the windows, trusting the security bars to keep me safe. The sheer silver curtains billow, the night breeze refreshingly cool.

As my bedroom, formerly a storage closet, has no windows, I leave the door open and drape the garment bag over a metal folding chair. The only other items in the small space are a twin-sized mattress, the matching box spring, and a suitcase filled with my clothes and other worldly belongings.

I've had less and I don't need more. That's what I tell myself anyway. I set the tote on the floor beside my bed and I undress, choosing to sleep naked, Blaine's key my only adornment, the ribbon soft against my neck.

I remove the beautiful white marble dildo from the black velvet bag. The stone is smooth and cool and I yearn to rub it all over my body.

I resist this temptation, as Blaine's instructions are clear. I'm to slide the dildo inside me. I'm not to touch myself or find release without him.

I lie back on the bed and spread my thighs. Blaine's scent surrounds me, clinging to the marble and to my body, dried cum flaking on my stomach.

I feel as though he's here. He's watching me. I push the dildo into my tight pussy, the hard marble stretching me open, the tip stroking my inner walls.

I reluctantly release the dildo, leaving Blaine's beautiful gift inside me. I imagine it's him inside me, his cock throbbing, filling me, and I sigh with contentment, closing my eyes.

Chapter Three

I DREAM I'M lying naked on the long wooden table in Blaine's office. My arms and legs are spread and my knees bent. I can't move, my limbs too heavy. The room is filled with men in dark suits, smoking cigars and swirling cognac in crystal glasses.

Blaine invites them, one by one, to look at me. The men bend their heads and peer between my thighs, gazing at my wet pussy. They grunt their approval. Blaine pokes and prods me, pride and some deeper emotion, an emotion I'm not brave enough to name, reflecting in his green eyes.

I wake up wet and aroused, my sheets soaked with perspiration. The dildo slides out easily, the marble slick with my juices. I feel empty and achy, my pussy missing the hardness, the fullness.

It's a struggle not to touch myself sexually in the shower, but I resist this temptation, skimming a washcloth over my body quickly. I leave the conditioner Blaine gave me in my hair, the vanilla scent covering my musk.

I wear the vintage purple Yves Saint Laurent two-piece skirt suit. The sleeveless vest sports a front closure, the three-quarter-length flared skirt can be flipped up, and the fabric is thick enough to conceal my taut nipples.

I grab my tote, slip my feet into my flats, and leave the house, wondering when I started choosing my clothing based upon how easy the garments are to have sex in. And I will have sex today, my need for Blaine undeniable.

First, I have to survive the day. I can do this. I'm strong . . . or so Blaine claims. I smile at the bus driver as I pay my fare. He straightens in his seat and smiles back.

I sit beside a heavily made-up, soaked in perfume woman. She gives me a haughty sniff, wrinkling her powdered nose, and continues talking loudly on the phone. She tells someone she calls girlfriend how all of the good men are taken, leaving only broke ass brothers for her to date.

The strip of turf has been replaced in front of Feed Your Hungry's headquarters. The sprinklers soak my shoes as I pass, the scent of freshly mowed grass and rich dark earth filling my nostrils.

I enter the converted house that was added to the main building, and the constantly texting receptionist says good morning to me. She reminds me cheerily that I have a meet and greet this afternoon with Mrs. Williams . . . as though I would ever forget. Securing a meet and greet with a donor is the goal of every Feed Your Hungry employee.

I wish I could say I legitimately landed this meet and greet. I didn't. Mrs. Williams agreed to donate money because she thinks I'm Michael Cooke's girlfriend. When I told her Michael and I were merely friends, the socialite didn't believe me and insisted on coming into Feed Your Hungry to personally drop off her donation. I couldn't say no, as this will only be the second donation I've secured. I need it to save my job.

I lie to everyone except Blaine, and if bending the truth allows me to keep my job at Feed Your Hungry, I'll bend the truth. I don't want to rely solely on Blaine's generosity and my evening job at his company. I prefer to pay my own way, maintaining at least the illusion of independence. I have my pride.

I pick up my donor list for the day from Feed Your Hungry's receptionist. All of the donors I am to call have given donations within the past year. My spirits lift. I might have a chance at securing a real meet and greet today.

I swing through the doors separating the new front addition from the original building and the temperature immediately rises. No one can recall the last time the air-conditioning in the older rooms worked.

I hurry along the hallways. The walls are painted a dreary gray, the plaster chipped. The carpet is frayed and thin.

I enter the large back room housing the pit. Rows of metal folding tables dominate the area, many of the seats already filled. My coworkers are dialing, their faces blank and their eyes glazed.

I slide into my chair in the back row and Goth girl, my

green Mohawk wearing friend, curls her black-lipstick-covered lips, giving me her version of a smile. She's wearing her usual black corset, black full skirt, torn mesh stockings, and clunky army boots, and is talking in sweet tones to a past donor.

I plug my headset into the flesh-colored telephone and dial and dial and dial. No one answers. Voice mail. Voice mail. Doesn't speak English. Voice mail. No one answers.

My fingers fall asleep. My thoughts turn to Blaine and the relentless throbbing between my legs. I'm aroused, needy. I press my thighs together. I won't last. I can't last. I wiggle.

"What's wrong with you, moth?" Goth girl stage whispers. "Do you have crotch critters or some other vagigi funkiness?" Heads turn and my face heats. "There's a free clinic close by. Ask Boss man for the morning off."

"I'm fine." I add another lie to my collection.

"Sure you are." My friend snorts.

She's right. I'm not fine. At noon I leap out of my chair, sling my tote over my shoulder, palm my phone, and hurry down the hallway, looking for a private place to make a call to a very wicked CEO.

"Hey kiddo. Are you looking for me?" Michael Cooke steps into the hallway and beams at me, his movie-star good looks dazzling. He's wearing a blue shirt that perfectly matches his eyes and clings to his wide shoulders. This designer garment is paired with khaki pants and Birkenstocks, two staples in the blond behemoth's wardrobe. "You have the meet and greet with Mrs. Williams today, don't you?"

"Yes," I reply, obliged to make polite conversation. Before I met a certain naughty billionaire, I dreamed of talking to Michael. Now it's a chore. Blaine is the sole man I want to speak with, to be with.

"Don't be scared about this meet and greet." Michael moves closer to me and I force myself to remain still, to not take a step backward. "Mrs. Williams is a close friend of the family, one of my honorary aunties, and I told her to treat you well, that you're special to me." He rubs my bare arms, his palms soft. "You are special to me, kiddo." He pushes his hips against mine and my body screams a silent protest. He's handsome and nice but he's not the man I want. "I wouldn't wait for anyone else."

Oh Lord. He's waiting for me to change my mind. I thought we talked about this. "We agreed to just be friends," I squeak, backing away from him.

Michael drops his hands. "We're just friends . . . for now." His face hardens and I put more distance between us. He's larger and stronger than I am and I don't trust him. I don't trust anyone except for Blaine.

Michael forces a smile, his teeth straight and white and perfect. "Will I be seeing my friend at lunch?" His gaze drops to my small breasts, my nipples remaining taut from Blaine's teasing.

"I'm not able to have lunch with you today." I edge toward the door. "But I'll talk to you later," I promise, eager to escape, to find the true source of my frustrations. "I have somewhere I need to be right now." I rush away, leaving Michael gaping after me.

I exit the building, turn into the employee parking lot and press redial. It rings twice.

"Anna." Blaine's deep voice makes my lower body clench. "What's wrong?" Voices chatter in the background.

"You know what's wrong." I pace on the uneven pavement, striding back and forth, seeking to expend some of my sexual energy. "What did you do to me?"

Blaine chuckles. The background voices fade and then disappear. "What did I do to you?"

"You know what," I fume, my need for him building with every passing minute. "I can't last."

Darla, Michael's big breasted blond friend, shimmies out of a cute little silver sports car, a vehicle no Feed Your Hungry employee could afford on our minimum wage salaries, and she walks toward me, a shiny red designer purse hanging from the crook of her right arm. As she spots me, she removes her overly large sunglasses. Her big brown eyes are wide with curiosity.

I don't want to talk to her. Darla is Michael's friend, not mine, and I don't trust her either. I don't trust myself right now, lust ruling my brain.

I turn my back, pretending not to see her, and I walk away, placing my hand over my phone. "I need to fix this. Now," I inform Blaine, my patience strained by need. "Either give me permission—"

"You do *not* have permission," Blaine barks, and my spine snaps straight, my body responding to his dominance. "I'll be there in five minutes." The phone clicks and the dial tone buzzes.

I can wait five minutes for sexual fulfillment . . . I think. I slip my phone into my tote. No, I know I can wait. I'm strong. I can do this. I gaze up at the blue cloudless sky and I wiggle, dancing in place, my blood singing with desire and need.

"She ran out the door like the hounds of hell were after her. It was the strangest thing." Michael's voice reaches me.

If Michael sees me, he'll want to talk to me again, and I'll then say something I'll regret, my mind focused on my arousal. I duck behind the building, wedging my body between a navy blue Dumpster and a red brick wall. A ghostly white moth flutters into the air, startled from her resting place.

"*She* is the strangest thing," Darla quips. "I saw her talking on her phone near the employee parking lot. I didn't hear her, but from her expression it appeared as though she was having boyfriend troubles."

"She doesn't have a boyfriend. Kiddo and I have an understanding," Michael says and I cringe, his words implying our understanding is we're more than friends.

"Do you? How cute." Darla laughs, the brittle sound holding more malice than joy. "She's a woman, Michael. She lies. I'll bet my favorite handbag she's seeing someone else and is playing you for a fool."

"She's not like that." Michael's voice fades. "She wouldn't lie to me."

I'm exactly like that. Guilt mixes with my desire. I am seeing someone else and I do lie. I smooth my long purple skirt. Even my clothes are a lie, Fran's designer suit not representing my true income. I knock a loose piece of brick off the wall, the gray mortar crumbling. Michael can't truly care for me because he doesn't know the true me. I only show myself to Blaine.

A black car approaches and I rush toward the busy street. The car is a sedan, not a limousine, and it passes without slowing down. It isn't Blaine. My shoulders slump.

The sun's rays beat down on my bare skin, its touch like a thousand fingertips. I shouldn't have called Blaine. I'm stronger than this, stronger than my body. My breasts ache and my pussy hums, my need dampened by guilt and disappointment but not extinguished.

A limousine slows and the back door opens. "Get in, nymph," Blaine orders. His suit is as black as his vehicle, his shirt a stark white. His purple tie matches my dress's shade exactly, and my spirits lift. We look like a couple.

I climb into the vehicle, the door closes, and Blaine grabs my wrist, pulls me to him, captures my lips with his, the force of his embrace driving my head back. I drop the tote and gasp. He surges into my mouth, his tongue filling me. Opening to him, I slide into his lap, straddling his thighs, clasping his shoulders.

Our tongues tumble and twist, his desire feeding mine. He wraps his arms around my waist, his palms flattening on my back, the warmth of his skin felt through the fabric.

This is what I need. "Yes." I arch my back and Blaine mouths along my neck, the pressure exquisitely firm. I unbutton my vest, wanting his touch on my bare breasts.

Blaine covers my fumbling fingers with his hands, his grip firm. "Not now." He raises his head, his eyes darkened to the deepest black. "I have no control."

I inhale, count to five and exhale. "I don't want you to have control." I slip the buttons through the holes. "I want all of you, Blaine."

He stills, his muscles tensing under me. "Are you certain?"

I nod and remove my vest, unhook my bra, undressing quickly, trying to outrun my fear. Will this change everything? Will he still want me after this?

Blaine tugs on his tie and pulls the strip of purple silk over his head. He shrugs out of his jacket, unbuttons his crisp white shirt, revealing golden skin and silver scars, the marks a physical reminder that he's faced adversity in the past and survived.

I retreat to the seat across from him, strip off my skirt and my white cotton panties. Will I soon be part of his colorful past? He must be accustomed to sophisticated, experienced women, women who don't associate sex with love, with trust.

"Anna." Blaine is naked, his cock hard, his legs long and firm and strong. "How does this make you feel?"

His question, a question he has asked me in the past, brings me comfort. "Scared." I give him a shy smile and the shameful truth. "I'm trusting you with everything." I'm trusting him with my body, my heart and my soul, risking a heartache I know I'll never recover from.

"Come here," he commands, his voice firm.

I kneel in front of him, naked, my gaze downcast and

my fingers shaking as I toy with the gold key between my breasts.

"Sit down."

I rise and straddle him, my bare skin sliding along his, my soft curves meeting his firm muscle. No barriers remain between us. I'm vulnerable, defenseless.

Blaine holds my face between his big rough hands and tilts my chin upward, the contact reassuring me. "I won't ever hurt you, Anna." Our gazes meet and hold, a connection stronger than words, stronger than our individual souls, binding us together.

"You won't leave me?" I ask, knowing the answer, needing to hear it again.

"Never." Blaine brushes his lips over mine. "You're my present and my future, my forever." He leans his forehead against mine. "I can wait forever if you need that time, Anna. This is too important to rush."

"I can't wait forever," I whisper. "I want you inside me. I'm just scared. I've never done this before and you . . . you have." He's a billionaire, a successful attractive man. He's probably slept with many glamorous women, women who know things, things I haven't even read about.

"Ahhh . . ." Blaine nods as though he understands. "I've been tested. I'm clean." He slides his right hand along the leather seat and holds up a blue package. "But this is your decision." He places the condom package in my palm, folding my fingers over it. "If it makes you feel less scared, use it."

"Oh." I stare at my hand, my mind spinning. "We have to use a condom. I'm not on birth control."

Blaine raises his eyebrows. "Do we have to use a condom?"

"Of course." I frown. "If there are any ... ummm ... consequences, you'll think I trapped you." That would be worse than stealing. I'd mess up his entire life.

His eyes soften. "I dream of those consequences." He splays his fingers over my stomach, his touch thrillingly possessive as though I already carried his child, our child. In Blaine's eyes, I see a future so precious I don't dare to believe in it.

"And I've been trapped for months," he adds, his tone filled with a quiet satisfaction. No one traps Blaine unless he wants to be trapped. Warmth spreads over my chest. He wants to be trapped by me.

"But this is your choice, Anna." He releases me and reclines on the lowered seat, his emotions hidden behind the mask he wears with others.

I turn the condom package in my hand, feeling the thin edges. I want a family, a child, Blaine, and a love without barriers, without fear. Am I brave enough to reach for what I want? "Is sex better without a condom?"

Blaine's eyes gleam. "I've heard it is."

"You've heard?" I meet his gaze, surprised. "You've never had sex without a condom?"

"Never."

This will be a first for him too. I'll be his first. I nibble on my bottom lip, intrigued by this possibility.

"Use me as you'd use your dildo." Blaine wraps his fingers around the base of his cock, offering himself to me, giving me all of the power. "My body is yours to control."

The condom package falls to the carpet, my decision made. I'll be his first. Wiggling forward, I push my wet pussy lips against his hard shaft, savoring the feel of soft skin over rigid steel. This is natural. This is right.

I lean over Blaine, placing hands on his chest, and I rock, building my confidence. We've done this before and I know how to move to please him, what he likes, what we both like.

"Cup my ass," I instruct, the authority in my voice surprising me. Blaine's lips curl upward and he lifts me, gliding my pussy up and down his cock, wetting his skin with my moisture, branding his flesh with my scent.

I ride his shaft, fucking him without entry, spiraling my want and need upward, no room in my mind for anything other than Blaine, his hands on my curves, his shaft pressing against my pussy, his musk, his heat, his suppressed desires.

Blaine's legs bounce under my ass and his jaw juts. These are the only indications his renowned restraint is compromised, and they aren't enough, not nearly enough. I graze my fingernails over his stomach and his muscles ripple. I want him as wild as I am.

As I rock, my hair falls forward, the tendrils teasing his chest. Blaine sucks in his breath, his eyes widening. I smile, having discovered another way to drive him crazy. I sweep the strands over his skin, caressing him with my hair, and a growl rolls up his chest. His cock bobs and his grip on my ass tightens.

He wants me badly and he can't do anything about it. He's trapped by his promise, Blaine too honorable to ever break a vow. I graze my fingers across his cock head, spreading the pre-cum over his shaft, and he shakes.

"Anna," Blaine rumbles.

He won't last and I want him inside me. "Lift me above you." As Blaine complies, I curl my fingers around his shaft, positioning him at my entrance. "Lower me slowly."

His cock head prods my pussy, pushes inside, stretching me. I muffle a moan, gripping his arms. He's broad, broader than anything I've ever taken. His tip slides up me inch by delicious inch, the fit agonizingly snug.

"Too tight," Blaine huffs, perspiration streaming down his angular face, his lips pressed into a grim white line.

"I can take you." Pain edges my voice. I grit my teeth as I continue the slow descent, his cock filling me. Have I told my first lie to Blaine? Can I take him? He's large, too large. Oh Lord. I dig my fingernails into his forearms. "I can't—"

My pussy lips touch his base and the slide stops, the fullness sublime. I'm impaled fully on his shaft, seated on my billionaire lover.

My lover . . . I'm no longer a virgin. I meet Blaine's gaze, needing his reassurance.

"You're perfect." His green eyes glow, the veins lifted on his forehead, his black hair damp. "You're made for me, Anna." Blaine holds me in place, his hands clamped on my hips.

We remain locked together. My body slowly adjusts to his girth, my grip on his cock loosening, the pain dissipating, leaving only desire. I shift and he sinks deeper. We both groan, our sexual satisfaction now coupled.

Blaine trembles, the strain of not moving, of giving me total control, reflecting in his face. I've allowed him inside me and my world didn't fall apart. I remain Anna Sampson, daughter of a dead thief and a runaway housewife, lover of the most trustworthy man I know. Blaine believes I'm strong, and I am strong enough to let go, to give myself over to him completely.

"I want you on top me, Blaine." I've dug red crescent moons into his forearms and I smooth the marred skin with my fingertips. "I want you to fuck me hard and fast, not holding anything back. I want you to fill me with your cum."

Blaine meets my gaze as though seeking confirmation. I nod, unable to repeat my instructions.

"Yes." He flips me onto my back and braces his body above mine, his weight heavy, comforting. I bend my knees, cradling him between my thighs, and I run my hands over his back, relishing his muscles, his strength.

Blaine pulls his hips back, brazing his cock head along my inner walls, and he pushes inside me once more, rocking my body. He repeats the action, moving slowly, allowing me to grow accustomed to him, and I undulate under him, caressing him with my breasts, my hips.

"Anna," Blaine rumbles. His shoulders flex under my fingertips, his form pulled tight, the shallow fucking testing his restraint.

He's been tested enough. "More, Blaine. Give me more." I wrap my legs around his waist and hook my ankles over his clenched ass, digging my heels into him, urging him to thrust faster, deeper.

Blaine increases his tempo, each drive forward bringing more pleasure, more connection, and once I learn his rhythm, I lift my hips, meeting him halfway, our bodies smacking together, heating my skin. He grunts, pumping into me, his face buried in my shoulder, his hot breath blowing along my collarbone, pushing my passions higher and higher.

I drag my fingertips over Blaine's back, leaving red trails over his muscles, marking him as mine. I'll be the first woman he comes in and the last. I'll be his only. A wet sheen covers his finely honed form and his male musk fills the air. He's inside me, this powerful man. He belongs to me. A savage lust, need, want rises in me.

"Claim me, Blaine." I squeeze him with my inner muscles and a strangled sound escapes his lips, muffled against my skin. "Claim me as I claim you. Make my body yours." I propel my hips upward and he drives me back, slamming my ass against the leather seat. We struggle, fight for fulfillment.

"Be still." Blaine nips my bottom lip. I nip him back, biting his lip and pulling. "Anna." He subdues me, thrusting into my mouth with his tongue and into my pussy with his cock, owning me, propelling me ruthlessly, relentlessly, toward the sharp edge of desire.

His body hardens even more, the firmness exciting me. I need—

He varies his angle, rubs over my clit, and I break, screaming into his mouth, arching, bucking, writhing, needing him closer, pushing him away. Waves of hot and cold sweep over me, the lights flashing. I clench my pussy down on his cock.

Blaine jerks, throws his head back and roars, temporarily deafening me, his face fierce, his eyes wild. Hard spurts of hot cum jet into me and my pussy muscles convulse. He thrusts once, twice more, holds a rigid pose for three heartbeats, his muscles staining, then he collapses, pinning me to the seat.

I squeak a protest, squished by his big physique, and Blaine rolls, murmuring an apology. He takes me with him, our bodies remaining joined, and he palms my bare ass, nuzzling his chin into my hair. I rest my left cheek on his skin, riding his heaving chest. His breathing gradually slows, his cock softening inside me.

We don't talk. We don't need to talk, both of us knowing words lie but bodies never do. The limousine vibrates under us. I don't know where we're going. I glance at the partition between us and the driver. It's closed.

"This first time is between us." Blaine presses his lips to my furrowed forehead.

This first time. I smile. He isn't taking what he wants and leaving. He's still here, holding me, talking about the future.

"How long do I have you, nymph?" Blaine smoothes my eyebrows with his thumbs. "There's a dinner this evening I must attend but I can cancel the rest of my meetings."

I blink, touched he'd cancel meetings for me. Blaine has been working on a buyout of a New York rival for months, the deal close to being finalized. I know how important these meetings are to him and to his company.

"I can't cancel my meeting," I tell him. Canceling a meet and greet for any reason other than death results in an immediate dismissal from Feed Your Hungry. "I have to be back by two." I nibble on my bottom lip, thinking of my other commitments, wishing I could spend the day with Blaine. "I also told friends I'd go out with them between the two jobs. Do you want to join us?"

Blaine threads his fingers through my hair, gentling separating the tangled strands, his touch soothing me. "Why do you want me there?"

I sigh. He knows me scarily well. "There's a guy. He's a friend but . . ." I can't finish my sentence, the words feeling like a betrayal.

"He wants to be more." Blaine's lips twist. "If I join you and he doesn't know about me, you'll hurt him, Anna. You'll lose him as a friend."

He's right. I frown, dreading the conversation I must have with Michael. "I don't tell him anything, but I don't want to hurt him."

"I know you don't." Blaine curls a lock of my hair around his index finger. "I'll meet your friends some other time." He gazes at me as though I've given everything he's ever wanted. "And you'll meet mine."

I tense. Blaine accepts me as I am but will his friends? "Will they like me?"

"Yes," Blaine answers without hesitation, no doubt in his voice. I raise my eyebrows. "You won Fran over, nymph." He taps the tip of my nose and I blink. "She's my most fierce protector."

He tells me stories of how he met his other friends. I memorize names, hoping to make a good impression on them when we meet. We linger in the limousine, our moving oasis, as long as we can before dressing.

"Do I look different?" I tug on my vest, pulling the fabric tighter over my small breasts. Blaine's scent lingers on my skin, the soreness in my pussy attesting to our activities. I feel different, more confident and womanly.

Blaine's eyes glitter. "You look beautiful." He knocks on the window with his knuckles and the door opens. "Be a good girl, Anna." He brushes his lips over mine. "I'm watching you."

Not everything has changed. I smile as I exit the limousine.

The driver, Ted, smiles back. "I'm happy for the two of you, miss." He tugs on the brim of his flat black hat.

My face heats. He knows Blaine and I had sex. I *must* look different.

Chapter Four

I HURRY INTO Feed Your Hungry's head office and the receptionist glances up from her phone. "Your two o'clock meet and greet just arrived. She's in Meeting Room One."

Meeting Room One is the dominion of Melinda Grack, the queen of the big-breasted blondes. I run, frantic to limit the time Mrs. Williams spends with her. I rap my knuckles on the door and enter.

"There she is." Melinda Grack stands, her breasts threatening to pop out of her skintight sky-blue suit. "We thought we'd lost you, Anna." Her dagger-length nails dig into my arms as she drags me forward.

"Anna." An older blonde rises to her six-inch heels. Her skin is pulled tight over her cheekbones, giving her a catlike appearance. I stiffen, recognizing her. I saw her once having coffee with Michael and his mother. "I *can* call you Anna, can't I?" she purrs, extending her perfectly manicured fingers.

"Yes, of course." I grip her hand. Her handshake is limp, her skin sickly soft. "It's a pleasure to meet with you, Mrs. Williams."

"The pleasure is all mine, Anna. We're going to be good friends, you and I." She sits once more, her white sheath dress resembling the garment Michael's mother had worn. I choose the seat beside Melinda and gaze at Mrs. Williams warily, her friendliness too exaggerated to be real.

The air-conditioning hums, the temperature chilly. The last time I was in this room, I was positioned on the table, lying on my back, naked, with Blaine between my spread thighs. I tug at the collar of my purple suit, my clothes suddenly feeling restrictive.

"Melinda, if you would be a dear." Mrs. Williams's tone smacks of condescension. "And grab me a bottle of water, Icelandic red only, please." She flattens one of her palms above her generous breasts and flutters her fingers. "My system is delicate." The lies roll off her tongue.

"Of course." Melinda is forced to agree, her expression as brittle as glass. "I'll get you a bottle right away." She glances pointedly at me, telling me without words not to mess this up, and she saunters from the room, her hips swaying.

Mrs. Williams closes the door. "Irritating ingratiating creature." The widow's smile fades and I tense, bracing for a verbal assault. "And who are your people, Anna? I asked around L.A. society and no one has ever heard of you."

As I consider which lie to give her, she circles the

small space, stops in front of the fake ficus and flicks a leaf. Dust motes swirl in the air and Mrs. Williams's unnaturally straight nose wrinkles with disdain.

This is how she'll look at me if she ever found out about my father. I touch the black ribbon encircling my neck, drawing confidence from Blaine's key. "I don't have people. I'm no one."

"Is that why Michael is interested in you?" The aging blonde turns to face me, her white designer dress contrasting vividly against the beige walls. "Because you're no one?"

I shrug, not knowing why Michael is interested in my public persona. I never show him the real me, as I don't trust him not to hurt me. "We're only friends."

"You're not only friends." Mrs. Williams glares at me. "Michael cares for you . . . deeply, and I should know his feelings. His mother is my best friend, I held him the day he was born and I helped bandage his scraped knees. He tells me everything, things he doesn't tell his own mother."

"You love him." Envy swirls deep in my soul. Michael has two mothers who love him, who would fight to protect him. My mother didn't fight to protect me. When my father went to prison, she walked away from him, from me, leaving me to face the world alone.

"Of course I love him." Mrs. Williams approaches the table. "And I won't allow a lying social climber such as yourself to hurt him. Michael deserves better. He deserves someone who loves him for himself, not for his money or his connections."

"I agree," I say quietly, gripping my hands under the concealing tabletop. "I don't love him. That's why we'll never be anything more than good friends."

"You agree?" Mrs. Williams sits down, appearing stunned. "But Michael is good looking, wealthy—"

"He's also a wonderful person and has a great sense of humor and most of the women working here are in love with him." I smile gently, aware that any normal woman would be lusting after Michael. I'm not a normal woman. "I'm not in love with Michael. I'm in love with someone else."

As the words leave my lips, I stare at Mrs. Williams, realizing they aren't lies. I love Blaine.

"Oh." Mrs. Williams blinks her catlike eyes.

"Oh," I repeat, equally dumbstruck. I love Blaine. I truly love him. I rub my hands together, my feelings both thrilling me and scaring me.

"You must think I'm a fool." Mrs. Williams twists her lips.

"I don't think you're a fool," I protest. "Just the opposite. You're trying to protect your best friend's son. I find that admirable." I pat her cold hands.

"You do?"

"It's very admirable." I nod. "We should protect the people we love." I didn't understand this before but I do now. I love Blaine and I'll do anything to keep him safe, to make him happy.

Silence stretches. Mrs. Williams gazes at me as though I'm supposed to say something. "Do you want to know what Feed Your Hungry does?" I ask.

"No." Mrs. Williams spreads her fingers, examining her immaculate nail polish. The tips of her nails are perfectly shaped.

I tuck my fingernails under my ass and try to remember the training. Somehow I have to move us to the exchange of money stage. I can't remember how and I suspect I'm on my own.

"Melinda is never coming back, is she?" I guess.

Mrs. Williams grins, genuine humor lighting her eyes. "There's no such thing as Icelandic red water."

I tilt my head toward the widow, one liar acknowledging another liar's prowess. I want to ask if she'd loved her deceased husband, if she'd ever shown her true self to him, how badly had he hurt her and had loving him been worth it, but I remain silent. It's too late for me. I love Blaine, and if pain is coming, I can't stop it.

"I'll see you out, then." I scramble to my feet, needing to escape my thoughts.

"First, I'll give you this." Mrs. Williams removes a check from her white clutch purse and places it on the tabletop. The donation is more than a full year's salary. "And thank you, Anna." She hugs me, the embrace awkward.

"Thank you for supporting Feed Your Hungry." I walk her to the door. We shake hands one more time and Mrs. Williams leaves, squinting at the sun, appearing at peace and almost happy.

She faced me and found her fears to be unfounded. Perhaps my fears about Michael's reaction will be unfounded also.

I give the check to the receptionist, asking her to pass it to Melinda Grack. After I stress for the third time how important this check is, the receptionist rolls her eyes and adds it to an impressively thick stack of checks.

I take a deep breath, count to five, and exhale. This has to be done, now, before Mrs. Williams talks to Michael. He should hear about this from me.

I march through the doors of doom, turn the corner, and enter Michael's office. He's talking on the phone, his Birkenstocks propped up on his desk. The flickering fluorescent lights make his blond hair glow golden. His eyes are the color of a tropical sea. There isn't a scar on his handsome face. I've never seen a man so good looking.

I'm not attracted to him at all. Blaine heats my blood with one green-eyed glance. Michael kissed me and I felt nothing.

I shut the door, needing privacy for this conversation. My stomach spins. I haven't had a discussion like this before, having spent my life being invisible, not noticed by men, and I don't want to hurt him.

Michael sets his phone down on his desk and plants his feet on the frayed carpet. "What's up, kiddo?" He raises his eyebrows. "Did everything go okay with Mrs. Williams?"

"Yes." I swallow hard. "She loves you."

"She does," Michael replies casually, as though he assumes everyone loves him, not knowing how precious and rare love is.

Does anyone love me? Does Blaine love me? He protects me as Mrs. Williams protects Michael. Is that love?

"What's wrong?" Michael frowns. "Did Mrs. Williams say something? I'll talk to her." He reaches for his phone.

"No," I shout, and he stares at me, his blue eyes widening. "There's no need to talk to her. I . . . ummm . . . I cleared up the misunderstanding she has about me being your girlfriend." I talk to the space above his left shoulder, unable to meet his gaze. "I explained to her I'm in love with someone else."

"Clever girl." Michael barks with laughter, the booming sound filling the small space, echoing off the walls. "That will throw her off our scent."

Our scent. I shift my weight from my right foot to my left. "It's the truth, Michael. I love someone else."

"No, you don't love someone else." Michael shakes his head. "You'll love me . . . eventually. But there's no rush." He holds up his big palms. "We're taking it slowly, you and I, going at your speed."

"I love someone else," I repeat.

"Stop saying that!" He surges to his feet and I take a step backward, terror skittering up my spine. "Don't joke about this, Anna." Michael grasps my arms, his grip painfully tight. "And you have to be joking. We have an understanding."

"Our understanding is we're just friends." I gaze up at him, scared. He's bigger and stronger and I don't trust him, not like I trust Blaine. "That's all we are, all we'll ever be."

Heated emotion flashes in Michael's eyes. "Friends." He squeezes my arms harder and harder, my bones bending under his fingers. "I love you."

"Michael, please let me go." Fear strangles my voice, the pain intense. "You're hurting me."

"I'll let you go." He releases me and I sway on my feet, light-headed. "If that's what you want. Because I love you, and when we love someone we're supposed to set that someone free, aren't we?" His laughter contains no humor.

I want to disappear, to become invisible once more. Life was simpler then . . . and lonelier. I rub my arms, trying to erase the red marks, to erase Michael's anger. "I want to be friends."

"All righty, kiddo." Michael plunks his ass down on his chair, his smile not reaching his eyes. "I'm glad I could help you out with Mrs. Williams as a *friend*." He picks up his phone and turns away from me.

"I'm sorry, Michael," I whisper.

He doesn't say anything.

I hurt him even worse than he hurt me. I slink back to my seat in the pit.

Goth girl takes her headset off, her green Mohawk rattling. "You ditched me at lunch, moth." She bares her teeth at me.

"Are you angry with me too?" I gaze down at my list of past donors, miserable, my wonderful first time with Blaine now a distant memory.

"I'm not angry, fool." Goth girl knocks her knee against mine. "I was concerned." She sniffs the musty air. "Someone smells like expensive cologne and hot steamy sex. It wasn't Mr. Movie Residuals. He went out with his fellow trust fund babies. Oh." Her mouth drops open, revealing a tongue piercing. "You banged Gabriel Blaine."

"Shhh . . ." I hush her, glancing at Michael's office, not wanting to hurt him any more than I already have.

"Tell me he's as great as he smells," she whispers, bending her Mohawk topped head toward me. "And I'll be your faithful minion forever."

"You're outrageous." My lips twitch, my good mood returning.

"Yes, I am," Goth girl agrees. "And I won't stop bothering you until you tell me because we're friends and I should know."

I do want to be friends, real friends, with Camille aka Goth girl. I genuinely like her, and Blaine has proven to me at least one person in this world can be trusted. If there's one person in this world I can trust, there might be two.

"Come on, moth." My new friend digs her pointy elbow into my side. "Spill."

"Consider yourself my minion," I whisper.

"I knew it," Goth girl crows, smacking the metal tabletop with her ringed fingers. Heads turn. "What are you looking at?" she snarls and then laughs as the prissy looking brunette in the first row gasps.

"You're a menace." I shake my head and put my headset on. I dial endlessly. No one answers. Voice mail. Voice mail. Leave me alone. Voice mail. Hang up.

Goth girl lands a meet and greet, and I bask temporarily in her good fortune, genuinely happy for her. I don't connect with anyone on the list.

Five minutes before five o'clock Michael swaggers toward me, his smile strained. Two of his friends trail behind him. Darla looks gleeful, her blond curls bouncing and her big breasts thrust out. Spencer fiddles with his phone, boredom reflecting in his vacant eyes, his face red and his dark hair carefully styled to appear messy.

They'll tell me they don't want me to join them tonight. I tense, having faced this rejection whenever friends found out about my dad.

"Are you ready to go?" Michael doesn't meet my gaze.

Goth girl pushes her chair closer to mine. "I thought you'd never ask, lover." She flutters her fake green eyelashes.

"He wasn't talking to you, freak," Darla snaps.

Goth girl stiffens beside me, my rebellious friend not as uncaring as she appears. "How do you know he wasn't talking to me, Barbie? Does he clear all of his conversations with you first?"

"Shut up, Camille." Michael glares at Goth girl. "I *wasn't* talking to you, freak." His gaze drops to her cleavage. "I *never* am." Darla sniggers and Spencer smirks.

I straighten. "Michael—"

"No." He holds up his hand. "You want to be friends but this isn't possible if you insist on hanging out with her." Michael meets my gaze, his blue eyes ice cold.

In the past I would have buckled under the pressure, deserting Goth girl as my mother deserted me. "I insist on hanging out with Camille." I raise my chin, now knowing if I care for someone, I should protect her. I shouldn't run.

Michael rears back as though I struck him. "You're choosing *her* over me?"

"I'm not choosing anyone." I grit my teeth, angry with him for putting me in this position. "I consider both of you to be my friends."

"Fine. Then I'll choose for you." Michael pivots on his Birkenstock-clad heels and stalks away, his ass cheeks clenching and unclenching under his tight khakis. Darla hurries to catch up to him, hooks her arm in his and throws a triumphant smile over her shoulder. Spencer looks at me and then at Michael, shrugs and follows his friends.

"You *insist* on hanging out with me?" Goth girl's voice sounds suspiciously watery. "Wow, moth. I didn't know you cared."

"Yeah, well, good minions are hard to find." I grab my tote, needing to see Blaine. "I'm sorry for ditching you at lunch," I mutter as I leave the pit.

I ignore the group of women gathered in a corner of the room, looking at me with a mixture of disbelief, pity, and outrage, judging me. They don't know me. They only see what I allow them to see.

The receptionist has left for the evening, my check no longer on her desk. I step through the doors and blink, the sunshine surprising me. It's only five o'clock yet it feels like years since I returned from my long lunch with Blaine.

I walk to the bus stop and tilt my head back, gazing up at the blue sky. An airplane leaves a white trail behind it, its passengers knowing their destinations, their course chartered, their immediate futures set.

My phone rings and I search through my tote.

"Blaine." I cover my mouth with my hand, blocking some of the traffic noise. "Is everything okay?" I ask him the question he always asks me when I call him.

"Yes, nymph." Blaine chuckles, the low, deep sound arousing me. "Why aren't you out with your friends?"

"How did you know I'm not out with my friends?" I look around me, searching for my enigmatic billionaire. Bumper-to-bumper rush hour traffic streams along the street. Commuters gather on the sidewalk. "Are you watching me?"

A limousine turns the corner and slows in front of the bus stop. "I'm always watching you." The door opens and Blaine holds out his hand, a phone cradled by his ear. I grasp his fingers, relying on him to steady me as I enter the vehicle.

The door shuts and Blaine pulls me onto his lap, places his phone on the seat. I set my phone beside his, my tote falling to the floor.

Blaine runs his hands over my body as though needing to physically confirm I'm with him. He freezes, his fingers hovering above the marks Michael left on my arms, the bruises striping my skin.

"Someone dared to hurt you?" Blaine's body tenses, his muscles contracting under me. "Tell me his name." His voice becomes scarily soft, his eyes hardening to emerald chips. "I promise he'll never touch you again."

I shiver at the implied threat. Blaine always keeping his promises. "You won't harm him." I tilt my chin upward. "It was an accident. I told him I loved . . . cared about someone else and he grabbed me, temporarily forgetting his own strength. Once he discovered he was hurting me, he let me go."

"He grabbed you," Blaine growls, not commenting on my revealing slip of the tongue. "And he hurt you, Anna." He holds me close, his scent and body heat comforting me, his shoulders wide and capable. "I won't tolerate either of those actions. I can't. You're too important to me." He rubs his palms along my back, sending sweet sensations over my body. "When I find out who he is, I'll—"

"You'll do nothing." I meet Blaine's gaze, narrowing my eyes. "Because if you hurt him, he'll press charges and you'll go to prison. My father died in prison." My voice breaks. "I can't lose you too, Blaine. I just . . . can't." I look away from him, unable to contain my emotion.

"You won't lose me." He cups my chin, forcing me to meet his gaze. "We're growing old together, you and I." Blaine presses his lips to my forehead, his heated touch reassuring me. He's here, alive, and he'll remain alive. I'll protect him as he protects me.

I bury deeper into his hard form and he holds me, his suit-clad chest rising and falling against my breasts, the connection between us strong. He's my sanctuary in this harsh, unforgiving world, the truth in an endless abyss of lies.

"Where are we going?" I gaze up at him. Blaine's determination is etched upon his face, his angles sharper, more pronounced.

"I'm taking you to dinner," Blaine murmurs. "If you're able." He traces my bruises, his touch gentle and his expression stormy. "I don't want you seeing him again, nymph. He could have broken your arms."

"He didn't break my arms and I'm able to go to dinner." I wiggle, brushing my ass against his thighs, and Blaine's hands lower to my hips, some of his anger flowing to desire. "Is this a date?" I've never been on a date, a real date, before, having never trusted a man enough to choose to be alone with him.

"This is a business dinner, unfortunately." Blaine bends his dark head and scatters soft kisses over my arms. "Volkov and his wife are visiting from New York. He's stalling on the sale."

I wrinkle my nose. "Is the sale in jeopardy?" Blaine has been working on this New York deal longer than we've known each other. It's important to him and, as a result it's important to me.

"We can't give him any reason not to sell. Volkov is understandably nervous. This involves his life's work and his employees." Blaine picks up his phone and texts quickly, his fingers flying over the tiny keys. "I'm asking Yen to bring your shawl."

"My shawl?" I tilt my head. I don't own a shawl, my wardrobe extremely limited. Everything I own fits in one carry-on suitcase.

"I saw it in a boutique and thought of you," Blaine says gruffly. "I'll introduce you as Anna. Nothing much gets by Volkov. He won't believe you're my assistant."

"So I shouldn't lie to him." I nibble on my bottom lip, excited and nervous about our first public appearance as a couple.

"Don't lie to him or to his wife." Blaine runs his thumb over my abused flesh. "You'll be fine, nymph. Volkov and I will do much of the talking." He slides his hands under my skirt, hooks his fingers around my panties and pulls them down to my ankles.

"What are you doing?" I squeak, my pussy moistening.

"We've talked enough about Volkov." Blaine's lips lift, his eyes gleaming. "I'm the only one you should be concerned about." He strokes my bare legs. "And I want you bared to me."

I can give him what he wants. My skirt is long and Blaine will be by my side. I rest my head on his chest, drawing strength from his touch. He won't allow anyone to hurt me, to truly see me. He'll shield me with his presence, his big form.

The limousine slows and Blaine raps his knuckles against the window. The door opens. Blaine exits first and extends his hand. I grip his rough, callused fingers and he draws me to him.

I suck in my breath, fitting into his hard body. He's not handsome, he'll never be handsome, but he's striking, powerful, and mine.

Blaine links our fingers together and we navigate the busy sidewalk, people swarming around us. Grocers display exotic vegetables. Plucked clean ducks hang in store windows, their heads remaining attached. A white ceramic happy cat stares at us, its paw raised in greeting. The aromas of cooked meats and fragrant spices make my stomach growl.

We walk toward a small Chinese restaurant, one of

many situated along the busy street. The restaurant with its pavilion roof, multicolored neon lights, and red Chinese lanterns is magnificently gaudy. I recognize the name immediately.

"This is the restaurant you ordered from during your start-up years." I hug Blaine's arm. This is a special place for my self-made billionaire.

"We make all of our big announcements here," Blaine murmurs.

I'll be present during tonight's big announcement. I'll be part of his team, belonging. "I won't let you down." I cling to Blaine's hand as we approach the restaurant's glass doors.

A tiny Chinese lady clad in a tight-fitting navy blue suit steps forward, her straight black hair swinging over her shoulders. If it weren't for the five inch heels on her feet, she'd be my height.

"Mr. Blaine." She gives Blaine a curt nod. "You must be Anna." The lady smiles. She's gorgeous, her beauty marred only by a thin silver scar skimming along one of her cheeks.

"You must be Yen." I smile back.

"Ahhh . . . he has been talking about me, I see," the woman blusters, appearing more pleased than upset. "I'd say not to believe everything you hear, but you heard it from Mr. Blaine. Although he seldom volunteers the truth," she slides her glance to Blaine and shakes her head, "he doesn't lie." She holds out a finely woven black silk shawl. "This is for you." Yen's gaze drops to my arms and her eyes narrow.

"Mr. Blaine didn't hurt me." I quickly wrap the garment around my shoulders, covering my bruises. The material is sinfully soft, the design beautiful in its simplicity.

"I know Mr. Blaine didn't hurt you." Yen fixes her gaze on Blaine. "As your legal counsel, I'm advising you that it isn't self-defense if *you* kill him."

Blaine's lips flatten. "I didn't do anything . . . yet."

"It was nothing, an accident." I slip my fingers into one of his palms. "Accidents happen." I inwardly wince at my own cliché.

"If accidents happen again, make certain she pulls the trigger," Yen advises, her brown eyes glinting.

"You're not helping," I mutter. Yen laughs and Blaine's lips twitch.

We walk into the restaurant. The tantalizing scent of seasoned beef, roasted chicken, and steaming rice fills the air and my stomach rumbles. Heads turn, the drone of voices quieting. I step closer to Blaine and he squeezes my hand. I'm not alone. He's by my side.

A short round Asian man rushes forward, his face beaming. "Mr. Blaine." He bobs his head multiple times. "We are honored you chose Chinese Palace for this most auspicious occasion."

Blaine's face settles into a blank mask, all of his emotions hidden from others, from me. "We appreciate you reserving the restaurant for us on such short notice." He clasps the restaurant owner's hand.

A large distinguished man approaches, one of his arms wrapped around an equally tall brunette's waist, the woman's face lined with wrinkles, her hair too dark for her complexion to be natural. Both of them are dressed in black. I scan the room. Everyone is dressed in dark colors.

I spread my black shawl over my bright purple suit, seeking to look more professional, to not embarrass Blaine.

"What is this, Blaine?" The older man looks from Blaine to me, his pale blue eyes flashing with anger, and I tense. "Who is she?"

I try to pull my hand from Blaine's, expecting him to abandon me as others have abandoned me in the past. He tightens his grip, securing me to him.

"'She' is Anna, and you'll speak to her with respect, Volkov." Blaine shifts protectively in front of me, shielding me with his body.

"You talk to me of respect yet you keep her existence a secret?" the CEO of the New York–based rival company fumes. "I asked specifically about your family. When you didn't answer, I assumed you had no one, yet here she is and it's clear how much she means to you. What other secrets do you have? What other lies are you telling me?"

He's verbally attacking Blaine and I don't like it. I don't like it one bit. I glare at the big Russian, my body vibrating with anger.

"Why should I trust you with my company, with my own family?" Volkov's fingers fold into massive fists, his threat turning physical. "I was advised not to believe your promises, the promises of a common criminal, but like an arrogant old fool, I listened to my gut."

Blaine's body stiffens more and more with each word. He doesn't defend himself. He can't say anything, not without exposing me, and he's too honorable to do that.

"No." I'll defend him. I won't allow Blaine to be hurt because of me, because of my trust issues. I push under Blaine's arm and stomp toward Volkov, tilting my head up to meet his gaze. "You will *not* blame Blaine for keeping our relationship private." I poke the older man in the chest with my index finger. Volkov's eyes widen and his nostrils flare.

"And you will *not* question his word again, you hear." I poke Volkov again. He takes a step back. "Blaine's the most honorable man I know, the only being in this horrible hard world I trust."

"Anna," Blaine rumbles.

"Your company, your so-called family, has to earn *his* trust, not the other way around." I lift onto my tiptoes, clenching my fingers into fists, a lifetime of silently tolerating insinuations, of enduring veiled insults, of suffering pain, spilling out of my mouth in a torrent of words. "If they're anything like you, I doubt they're worthy."

Volkov's eyebrows lower and his weathered face darkens.

"Enough, Anna." Blaine hooks his arm around my waist and pulls me back.

I glower at Volkov, raising my fists, ready to beat some sense into the Russian's thick head. "I don't want him talking to you like that," I tell Blaine.

"I know. I know." Blaine turns me, burying my face

into his body. "He won't make that mistake again." His chest shakes.

"Are you laughing at me?" I scowl, wiggling, trying to free myself.

"He's a foot and a half taller than you, nymph. Of course I'm laughing at you." Blaine chuckles, holding me tightly. "You're crazy and fearless and absolutely perfect."

I stop struggling, content to be in Blaine's arms, my rage evaporating, defused by his scent, and he rubs my back, stroking his palms up and down, up and down, his chin resting on top of my head.

Chapter Five

As my anger fades, I realize what I've done. This dinner is important to Blaine and I've insulted and fought with the guest of honor. "I'm sorry," I mumble into Blaine's chest. "Have I ruined everything?"

"You've earned the undying loyalty of my team." Blaine kisses the top of my head. "They'll talk about this dinner for decades."

My crazy antics will be talked about for decades. That's not a good thing. I groan and Blaine's body shakes again. The situation can't be that serious if he's laughing at me.

"Are you ready to try this again?" he asks. I nod, the tip of my nose sliding along his silk tie. "Be a good girl, nymph." He releases me and says to Volkov, "I'd like you to meet Anna, the woman I protect as fervently as she protects me."

I count to five and reluctantly face the Volkovs. "I'm pleased to meet you, Mr. Volkov." I extend my hand, concealing my emotions.

The older man hesitates, his expression stern and forbidding. Mrs. Volkov slaps his back and Mr. Volkov grasps my fingers, his grip as firm as Blaine's. "I haven't had anyone question my worthiness in decades."

"Not to your face." I meet his gaze.

Volkov's lips quirk upward. "Not to my face," he concedes, dropping his hand. I force myself to stand still as he studies me for three heartbeats, his eyes as all knowing, all seeing, as Blaine's. He inclines his gray head slightly toward me.

"Your Anna may be your best acquisition yet, Blaine," Volkov declares, the skin around his eyes crinkling. His wife beams and the buzz of conversation resumes around us.

Volkov moves closer to Blaine. As the two CEOs talk in hushed tones, Mrs. Volkov stands silently at her husband's side. I smile at her. She smiles back and some of the tension eases out of my shoulders. I can do this. I stand beside Blaine, listening to the conversation, learning more about his business, about his challenges.

A very large man approaches us, his shoulders wide and his tread surprisingly quiet for his size. He's dressed from head to toe in severe black, his hair as dark as his suit, his tanned face somber and his chin square. He gazes at me with unblinking midnight eyes.

He's judging me and I'll be found wanting, as I always am. I glance up at Blaine. As I almost always am. I tuck my body into Blaine's hard form, yearning to disappear, to become invisible once more.

"Volkov, you've met Henley, my chief of cyber security." Blaine places his hand on my right hip, his grip gratifyingly secure. He's mentioned Henley, a man he trusts completely, advising me to contact him in case of an emergency.

"Of course we've met." Volkov scowls. The two men shake hands.

Of course they've met. I shift my weight from my right foot to my left. Everyone knows each other, except for me. I only know Blaine.

"Henley, this is Anna." Blaine draws me forward.

Volkov's bushy gray eyebrows rise. "You haven't introduced her to your team?"

"Anna." Henley clasps my hand with both of his. Welts line his palms. I meet his gaze, shocked, and his dark eyes glint. "Mr. Blaine hasn't told you about me, has he?" Although his voice is flat and his expression blank, I sense his sadness.

"He told me he trusts you completely." I squeeze his hand. "And that's enough for me."

Henley's eyes soften for a heartbeat before hardening once more. He straightens to his full formidable height. "I see." And I believe he does, Blaine's trust hard to earn.

"Ready to meet the rest of the team?" Blaine swirls his fingers into my hip, his massage sensuous and arousing. I nod and he steers me through the room, introducing me to his people, giving faces to the names he's previously mentioned.

Henley continues to watch me, his dark gaze tracking my movements. I glance over my shoulder, his perusal making me uneasy.

"I told him should anything happen to me, you're his responsibility," Blaine murmurs in my ear. "Henley takes his responsibilities very seriously." He plays with the fringes on my shawl. "He'll never touch you but he'll always be watching."

I understand the meaning behind Blaine's words. Henley will be one of the men watching us in the future. Arousal unfurls, swirling low in my body. "As you always watch me?" My nipples tighten, pressing against the soft cotton of my bra.

Blaine's lips curl upward. "Not now, nymph."

"Not here?" I ask. He doesn't answer and I tremble, his silence implying he'll take me here. My skin instantly becomes more sensitive, my body more aware of Blaine's. Every brush of his fingers is accentuated, every casual bump of his hips against mine amplified.

We sit at a huge round table covered by a bright red tablecloth. Blaine pulls our chairs close together, his thigh pressing against mine, his body heat warming me through the layers of fabric.

Platters of foods are set on a rotating tray in the middle of the table, and as Blaine continues a heated discussion with the business-focused Volkov, I transfer some beef teriyaki onto his plate. Mr. Lee, the hovering restaurant owner, nods his head, approving of my choice.

I eat quietly, content to listen to the conversations around me, remaining semi-invisible tucked close to

Blaine. He grazes his fingertips along my side, up and down, up and down, teasing me, tormenting me. I'm conscious of him, too conscious, my body yearning for his touch.

Blaine slips his hand under the tablecloth and slowly pulls my skirt upward, exposing my bare legs. I freeze, my fork raised in the air. Cool air wafts over my skin, exciting me.

He'll take me now, here. He prods his fingertips between my thighs and I open to him, spreading my legs, aware that anyone glancing under the table will see my wet pussy. They'll see my private curls, my pink folds, my tight, no-longer-virginal entrance.

Blaine caresses my skin, close but not close enough to my aching core, and I tremble, lowering my fork, passion's tremors radiating from his rough touch.

Henley, Blaine's serious friend, shifts, his chair creaking under his large form. He's seated across from us, watching me, his eyes as black as the night sky. Does he know Blaine has his fingers between my legs, that I'm being pleasured as we eat dinner?

I imagine he knows, that he watches as his boss finger-fucks me, that he wants to touch me also, his cock hard. It is a safe fantasy, as I know Blaine will never allow another man to touch me. I'm his, completely.

Blaine dips his fingertips into my wet heat and I jerk, the contact exquisite and forbidden. He strokes along my pussy, playing me as only he knows how, seducing me with his fingers.

I bow my head over my plate, concealing my face

behind my hair, unable to maintain my blank expression, wanting, needing, him too much. Blaine slides two of his fingers into my entrance, stretching my tender pussy open, and I bite my bottom lip, stifling my moan.

He maintains his conversation with Volkov as he pumps me, pressing the heel of his hand against my clit, the delectable pressure spiraling my need upward. I bring my cloth napkin to my mouth, muffling my pants. Perspiration drips down my spine.

I'm close, too close, my body coiling tight, my inner muscles gripping his fingers. Oh Lord. My thighs shake, the effort to remain still, to remain silent, tremendous. I'm going to come here, in a restaurant, while Blaine's business associates watch.

"Blaine," I whisper.

He leans closer, the heat of his body driving me ruthlessly toward fulfillment. "Come for me, Anna. Here." He plunges deep inside me. "Now." He curls his fingers and smacks the heel of his hand against my clit.

I buck upward, a cry torn from my lips. As I lose control, breaking into a million pieces, uncaring who sees or who hears, Blaine flings his arm out, knocking a full glass of water across the table. Women shriek and men jump to their feet. Waiters rush to soak up the mess.

Amidst the chaos, Blaine pins me to my chair. I writhe, the room spinning around me, my juices gushing over his fingers. He strokes along my inner walls, caressing inside me. Gradually, my heartbeat slows, my rational thought returning, and Blaine withdraws his hand, resting his wet fingers on my upper thighs.

"You're so responsive," he murmurs into my ear, pressing his cheek against mine. "And beautiful." Blaine nibbles on my earlobe, teasing my sensitive flesh. "And mine."

His employees return to their seats. Henley remains where he is, having never moved, his gaze fixed on us. He knows. I wipe Blaine's fingers with a cloth napkin, seeking to hide the truth from the others.

"Are we talking business?" Volkov grumbles. "I have an afternoon flight tomorrow."

"We're talking business." Blaine wraps his arm around my waist, tucking me close, and he turns back to the impatient businessman.

I glance across the table. Henley meets my gaze and tugs on the cuffs of his suit. I gaze down at Blaine's hands. One of his cuffs is pulled up, revealing his tanned wrist, his skin speckled with my pussy juices.

My face heats. I smooth Blaine's sleeve back down and Henley nods his approval, his face stern and his chin square.

He continues to watch me. I look around the table. Other people watch me, watch Blaine. They don't see all of me and they never will but I'm no longer invisible. I'm vulnerable, exposed, and until I develop another strategy to cope, I'll have to trust Blaine to protect me. I fit into his body, meshing my curves with his muscle, and his grip on me tightens.

As the night progresses, the conversations around us wane, and the waiters clean the table. One smiling waitress assures me no food is wasted, the leftovers are sent home with staff members. Men and women say their good-nights, returning to their homes, to their families.

Blaine and Volkov continue to talk, their heads bent and their tones serious. Mrs. Volkov sips coffee, her expression resigned, as though she's spent decades waiting for business talk to wind down. Every once in a while Volkov reaches over, squeezes her hand, and her face lights up.

They're a team, an aging patriarch and the woman who loves him. Mrs. Volkov isn't flashy. Her breasts are natural and her figure is soft. She also doesn't talk a lot. She's quiet like me. Talking isn't necessary. Volkov knows she's there, supporting him as he supports her.

I close my eyes, listening to the rumble of Blaine's voice, engulfed in his warmth. This is where I'm supposed to be also, by Blaine's side, supporting him, loving him.

I WAKE TO sunlight streaming through a window, the glass splitting the rays into a rainbow of colors. I frown, confused. My bedroom in the Leighs' bungalow doesn't have a window. As I try to sit up, a heavy band over my stomach prevents me from moving.

I look down at the tanned male arm strewn across my near naked body. Blaine lies with his face buried in a white fluffy pillow, his back bare, his ass clad in his boxer shorts. I'm wearing my white panties.

I stare upward, trying to remember how I got here. A gold framed mirror hangs on the ceiling, the contrast of my pale skin and Blaine's golden tan visually stimulating.

There's another mirror positioned at the foot of the bed, the wall behind it painted a warm brown. The furniture is rich dark wood, the four-poster bed intricately carved with vines and plants.

This is Blaine's bedroom, the space comfortable and right, designed for watching inhabitants at every angle. I breathe deeply, the room smelling of his cologne, of him.

It smells of me also. My suit is folded neatly on a chair beside the bed and my faux leather flat shoes are lined up underneath the seat, the matching tote leaning against a clawed foot.

Blaine turns his head and his gaze meets mine, his green eyes soft. "I didn't want to wake you." He strokes under my breasts and my nipples tighten, my body responding to his touch.

"I don't normally fall asleep in public places." I place his hand over my left breast. "And I don't normally wake up in strange beds."

"This isn't a strange bed. It's our bed." Blaine circles my nipple, teasing me, and I squirm, wanting more. "I'm meeting with Volkov at ten. How long do I have you?"

"I'm supposed to start work at nine o'clock." I need this job to maintain my independence and I should care about it. I can't summon up that concern, not right now, not while he's touching me.

Blaine shifts over me, his body heavy, solid, warm, pressing me into the mattress. "I'll give you a ride." He bends his head and swipes his rough tongue over my right nipple. I bow my spine, pushing my breasts into his mouth, his hand. He works me with his lips and his fingers, squeezing and releasing me.

"Will you give me a ride?" I lower my voice suggestively and run my hands over his flat pectoral muscles, across his cascading abdominal muscles. His stomach ripples. "Did you look at me last night? Did you touch me when you undressed me?" I explore his shoulders, the dip along his spine, the scars on his back.

"I wanted to do more than touch you." Blaine sucks on my nipple and I arch, crying out, the intensity sublime. "I wanted to fuck you while you slept." He swirls his tongue around the abused flesh, soothing me. "You were so still, so soft."

I was defenseless and vulnerable, and Blaine wanted me but he didn't take advantage of me. He kept me safe even from himself, respecting my boundaries and my fears.

"You can fuck me now." I slide my fingers under the waistband of his boxer shorts, his ass firm against my palms. "Taking me the way you wanted to take me last night." I push the soft cotton down and curl my fingers around his hard shaft. "Filling me." I run my hands up and down him.

"I *will* fill you." Blaine yanks on my panties and spreads my legs almost painfully wide, opening me completely to him. "You're wet for me, nymph." He rubs along me. "Hot."

"Always." I undulate, savoring the feel of his naked body against mine. "I'm always hot for you."

He lowers himself, pressing down on me, trapping me underneath him. I can't move, can't free myself, and once he enters me, he'll have me, seeing the needy piece of my soul I normally hide. He could hurt me as I've never been hurt before. I tremble, the old fears resurfacing.

Blaine pushes his cock head into my tight pussy. "Show me, Anna. Show me how much you want me."

I meet his gaze, seeing the understanding in his brilliant green eyes. He's offering me the gift of control, allowing me to give what other men might simply take. Blaine isn't other men. He's my man.

I lift my hips, taking him deeper and deeper and deeper, his tip sliding up me, stretching me. My pussy lips touch his base.

"This is how much I want you." I clench my inner muscles around him.

He groans and I grin, feeling powerful and strong. I lower. The retreat is as exquisite as the advance, desire flowing over me. I pump my hips up and down, fucking Blaine's huge cock as he remains still, braced above me, waiting for my command to move.

He'll wait forever, locked in place if I say nothing. I wrap my legs around him, pulling myself upward, savoring the glide of hard cock in wet pussy, boldly, ruthlessly using him for my own pleasure.

"You're so beautiful." His arms shake, veins lifting over his bulging biceps. Sweat beads on his forehead. He's suffering for me, my stubborn wonderful man, and I can't allow this.

"I'll show you everything, Blaine." I tilt my chin up, trusting him with all of me. "Fuck me hard."

"Yes." Blaine drives into me, covering my lips with his, filling my pussy with the entire length of him. I tighten my grip on his waist as he pounds into me again and again, thrusting with his tongue and his cock, slapping my breasts with his chest. My nipples, hips, lips hum.

I glance at the mirror hanging above us and watch the muscles in his back strain, his ass cheeks clench. He's superbly fit, Blaine's body a thing of beauty, and he's mine, all mine. I dig my fingers into his skin as he fucks me hard and deep, the bed shaking, sliding on the hardwood floor.

He doesn't hold anything back, his tempo fast and wild, his restraint stripped, leaving him bare, exposed. I meet each thrust, embracing his savagery. Only I see him like this, raw and stark and real, his face flooded with emotion, his eyes flashing.

He grunts, I pant, skin slaps against skin, the bed slams against the wall, our sex noises filling the quiet room, escalating my need. I ache. I burn. I break the skin on Blaine's shoulders, my fingernails digging into flesh.

I'm unrecognizable in the mirror, flushed and primal, a creature of passion. I'm no longer an innocent nymph skipping along a sandy beach. I'm a siren writhing on the jagged rocks, coaxing Blaine closer to his doom, intent on my own fulfillment.

He can give me what I need. I know this. "Blaine," I demand.

"Come for me, Anna. Here. Now." He bites my bottom lip, the pain splintering my soul.

I scream, light bouncing from mirror to mirror, criss-crossing the room, reflecting upon my heart. I drive my hips upward, taking Blaine fully inside me, and I tighten my inner muscles viciously around his shaft, mercilessly yanking his release from him, determined not to come alone.

"Anna," Blaine roars. He pushes even deeper, spurting hot hard jets of cum into my pussy, coating me with his essence. Swirling his hips, he grinds against my clit and I whimper, a second wave of almost unbearable pleasure sweeping over me. My pussy muscles convulse, milking him dry.

Blaine collapses on top of me, pressing me into the mattress, his weight heavy and right. I stroke his back as he shudders, his skin smooth, wet and warm.

He rolls onto his back, his expression gratifyingly dazed.

I look up at the mirror. My lips are swollen and red, my nipples tight. My pussy lips glisten with our combined juices. These juices also coat Blaine's cock.

"Is it always like this?" I meet Blaine's gaze in the reflection.

"No." He shakes his head, his denial immediate. "Never. Only with you, Anna." One of his palms cover mine, our fingers link together and we lie in bed, staring upward, watching each other.

The moment stretches, a moment I savor, hold in my heart, not knowing if there will be more moments like this. I took the moments I had with my parents for granted. I'll never do this with Blaine.

Somewhere within his house a clock chimes, the musical tones announcing the return of reality. I have bills to pay and other responsibilities.

I sigh. "I should get to work." I reluctantly roll out of bed and dress, not bothering to don my bra and panties, planning to shower and change next door.

I look around for the ribbon I always wear. "Have you seen my key?"

"I have it." Blaine stands behind me, clad in his white boxer shorts, his body muscular and hard. "Hold up your hair."

I gather the strands in my fingers he encircles my neck with the black ribbon, fastening the repaired clasp. Now two keys dangle between my breasts. The large gold key is for his backyard. I don't know what the small rhinestone bedazzled gold key is for.

I turn my head and gaze over my shoulder at Blaine. I lift my eyebrows.

"The diamond key is for our house." He shifts behind me, avoiding my gaze, my billionaire CEO appearing adorably nervous.

It isn't a rhinestone. I study the intricately crafted piece of jewelry. It's a very large diamond. And the key is for *our* house. I have a house, a permanent place to live, a permanent place by Blaine's side. I haven't had a home since I was fourteen years old. "It's beautiful." I blink back tears, emotion welling inside me.

"You're beautiful." He turns me to face him and tilts

my chin upward. His green eyes glitter. "All I have is yours, Anna. I'd give you the stars if I could."

"This key is as stunning as the stars and it is much more practical." Balancing on my tiptoes, I press my lips to his. "I love it." I love him. I'm not brave enough to say this. Blaine has never spoken of love and I won't be the first.

He hugs me to his near-naked body, his breath wafting on my neck, the keys trapped between us, warmed by our skin. "Damn Volkov," Blaine mutters. "Tonight, we'll celebrate." He hands me my tote, my bra and panties stuffed inside the bag.

"You'll smoke one of your cigars." I walk with him through the antique-filled house, the colors warm, the furniture solid wood. "And watch me as I swim naked in your pool."

Rich oil paintings decorate the walls, the scenes depicting waterfalls and butterflies and uninhabited landscapes. My shoes sink into the handwoven rugs.

"You'll swim naked in *our* pool," Blaine corrects me. We descend a winding staircase, the wrought-iron railings twisted into a vine and leaf design. "We'll make love under the stars."

We won't fuck. We'll make love. My chest warms. We enter a grand foyer. A huge crystal chandelier hangs over our heads. Blaine's bare feet smack against earth brown tiles.

As we wander to the front door, I slow our pace, gripping his fingers tighter, not wanting to leave him. "Blaine."

"Not now." He opens the door, uncaring that he's clad only in his white boxer shorts, his hair mussed and his body firm. "I'll be in the limousine waiting for you." He leans into me and brushes his lips over mine. "Come over when you're ready."

I'm ready now. I gaze at Blaine. I want him. I need him.

He chuckles. "Don't look at me like that, nymph. You have to go to work." He turns me, places his palm on the small of my back and pushes me gently out the door.

The sun's rays warm my skin. Birds chirp. The limousine waits in the driveway, Ted sitting in the front seat, staring down at his phone.

Blaine's schedule affects other people—Ted, his assistant Fran, any employees he has meetings with. They'll want to know where he is and wonder why he's late. They might guess what we were doing.

I hurry next door to the Leighs' modern bungalow. As I fiddle with the finicky front door lock, I check the mailbox. There aren't any letters or packages, not one piece of junk mail in the metal box. That's not unusual. The mailman has taken days off in the past.

I drop the key. As I bend to retrieve it, my heart clenches. A moth lies on the concrete steps, her wings broken and her body still. I pocket the keys and nudge her belly with my finger. She doesn't move.

I scoop the moth off the steps, cradling her in my palm, and transfer her to the grass, hoping the connection with nature will revive her. Brown powder transferred from her fragile wings cover my skin.

It isn't an omen. It isn't. My fingers shake as I insert the key. The lock clicks and I open the door, entering the hot house. Everything is in place, the store catalogues arranged perfectly on the glass hallway table, the geometric glass objets d'art Suzanna Leigh collects arranged on shelves, and the windows securely closed, the temperature already stifling.

Leaving my shoes at the door, I rush along the hallway, passing the life-sized photo of Mrs. Leigh, her blond hair, blue eyes, and big breasts representing what I previously thought every man wanted.

One man wants flat chested, brown-eyed, brunette Anna Sampson, and this won't change because a moth foolishly flew too close to a light, paying the ultimate price for her ambition.

I flip through the clothes Fran has given me and dress in the vintage chocolate brown Givenchy suit. The skirt has a fun kick pleat, the equestrian style jacket closely fitted. I wear a black tank top underneath the suit.

Normally, I'd carry the jacket in my tote and wear only the tank top, the combination too hot for the bus. Today, I'm sharing Blaine's air-conditioned limousine.

When I exit the house, I don't check on the moth's condition. I can't do anything more to help her, and if I don't look, I can tell myself she has recovered. She's fluttering happily in the green grass, not lying lifeless and stiff and alone.

I'm not alone. Blaine's keys clink together as I walk. I have a home, a permanent home, and a man who cares for me.

"Good morning, Miss Anna." Ted, the driver, smiles as he opens the door.

"Good morning, Ted." I climb into the limousine and the door shuts behind me. "Good morning, Blaine." I grin, settling into the seat beside him.

"Good morning, nymph." Blaine grins back. He's dressed in his usual black suit and white shirt. A happy yellow tie is tightly knotted under his pointed chin. His black hair is wet, his rebellious strands subdued. "Did you sleep well?" he asks with a grin, putting his arm around me, his cologne teasing my nostrils.

"I slept well and woke even better." I stretch, rubbing into him, the connection reassuring me. He's here. He won't ever abandon me. "I still feel you inside me," I whisper.

"No touching yourself during the day," Blaine instructs, tapping the tip of my nose with the index finger of his right hand. Light reflects off his yellow cuff links.

I frown, my uneasiness returning. "I won't see you at lunch?"

"Not today." Blaine kisses my forehead, his mouth hot. "I'm locked in meetings with Volkov. He finally reached a decision yesterday and now he wants this deal completed quickly."

"That's good news." I summon up a smile, knowing how much this deal means to Blaine. I'm strong. I sink deeper into his hard body, drawing comfort from his unyielding physique, his strength. I can wait until six o'clock to see him again.

Chapter Six

THE RECEPTIONIST LOOKS up from her phone as I enter Feed Your Hungry's lobby. "Your donor list is with your manager," she tells me gleefully, her eyes glittering with malice.

I'm in trouble. Clutching my tote tightly, I hurry to Boss man's office. The glass door is closed and so are his eyes, his head bobbing, his rounded chin tucked into his chest.

I knock and he jerks upright, his arms shooting outward. He nods at me and I enter. "I'm told you have my donor list?" I ask.

"Yes, yes." Boss man rummages through the paper on his desk and finds the donor list. He blinks a couple of times. "Anna," he adds, as though he'd forgotten my name. "After two months of working for us, you've only secured two meet and greets." He clucks his tongue.

Oh Lord. I'm getting fired. I square my shoulders,

bracing for the news. "One of the meet and greets was with a new donor to Feed Your Hungry," I remind him.

"Yes." Boss man frowns, his forehead wrinkling. "The board has concerns about associating with someone of Mr. Blaine's character."

"What?" I straighten.

"He's an ex-con, Anna." Beads of sweat form on Boss man's top lip. His brown hair is matted, sticking to his high forehead. "What would other donors think if they knew we accepted money from the criminal element?"

"Gabriel Blaine is not the 'criminal element.'" I stare in disbelief at my manager. "He went to prison for hacking and that was years ago, while he was at college."

"I also understand your second meet and greet was secured with help from another employee." Boss man ignores my heated defense of Blaine. "You're late today and you took an extended lunch yesterday. The board is questioning your commitment to Feed Your Hungry."

"I see." And I do see. This isn't about Blaine or my performance. I'm being punished for rejecting Michael Cooke, their superstar employee.

"I like you, Anna." Boss man sighs. "I do. You're different. And I want you to do well here."

I'm different. Michael said this about me also. I've never thought being different was a good thing. I've tried all of my life to be as normal as possible. "Thank you, sir."

"Do us both a favor and land a meet and greet today." Boss man hands me the donor list.

"I will, sir." I'll dial until my fingers fall off.

I scan the list as I swing through the doors of doom.

I've never seen such an obsolete list. None of the donors have contributed in the past three decades. Sweat trickles down my spine.

I pass Michael's office. He's leaning back in his chair, his hands linked behind his blond head, his Birkenstocks propped up on his desk. He meets my gaze and his blue eyes narrow.

"Stubborn ass," I mutter under my breath. An uptight brunette in the front row hisses at me. I glare at her. She covers her mouth as she whispers to the red-faced girl sitting beside her.

"Look at you, moth, working rich kid hours."

I turn my head toward the back row and I stare. The voice belongs to Goth girl. The face does not. Yes, her features are the same. She has the same ski jump nose, the same defiant chin, but her hair is black, pulled back ruthlessly into a tight ponytail, and she hasn't any piercings or tattoos. Her lips are painted a frosted girly pink and she wears a body-hugging black suit.

Goth girl looks normal, better than normal. I blink, trying to process this new side of my friend. She's beautiful.

"Don't say a word," she snarls, her brown eyes flashing, her tapping fingers devoid of rings.

"I wouldn't dare, *Camille*." I grin, hopeful. If Goth girl can rejoin the human race, I can land a meet and greet today and save my job.

"I did all of this for nothing." My friend drums her feet against the frayed gray carpet. She's wearing five inch black heels and has legs a supermodel would envy. "I con-formed for nothing."

"And here I thought you dressed like a human being for me." I remove my jacket and hang it on the back of my chair, my black tank top already drenched with moisture. "Where's my headset?"

"Mine is missing too." Goth girl rolls her eyes, her skillfully applied makeup natural rather than her usual theatrical look. "And my donor list is older than I am."

"I'm sorry," I mumble as I sit down, feeling horrible for dragging Goth girl into my drama. This is all my fault. I glance at Michael's office. I encouraged him, I rejected him, and now he's punishing both of us.

"Not as sorry as I am." Goth girl leans closer to me, her impressive cleavage threatening to pop the top buttons off her blazer. "I dressed this way for my meet and greet today, only to be told, even with the transformation, I didn't portray the proper Feed Your Hungry image." Her pink lips twist.

"That sucks." I bump my shoulders against hers. "But you should have warned me. I would have paid money to see the expressions when you walked in."

Goth girl grins at me. "That *was* worth it. I thought Michael Cooke was going to swallow his tongue." She cackles with glee.

I don't want to think about Michael. I pick up the flesh-colored receiver and dial, determined to land a meet and greet, to save my job, to prove the others wrong and Boss man right. I'm strong and intelligent. I work hard. I can do this.

No one is home. Voice mail. No one is home. I told you people to take me off this list. Click. Dial tone. Voice mail. She died twelve years ago. No one is home.

As Michael leaves for lunch with his friends Darla and Spencer, he glances over his right shoulder at me. His mouth opens and then snaps closed, his jaw jutting.

"Mr. Trust Fund isn't ready to forgive you quite yet, huh?" Goth girl pats my shoulder. "Don't worry. He'll come around." She struts to the kitchen, her walk as defiant as ever.

I know Michael will come around. They always come around. Then I break another social rule and they abandon me again, hurting me even more the second time. In the past I blamed myself for this cycle of pain and betrayal. I now realize they weren't strong enough to be my friends.

Having forgotten to bring a lunch, I dial the next number on the donor list. No one is home. Voice mail. Voice mail. This phone number is no longer in service.

I smile at Goth girl as she returns with her delicious smelling curry. She's put extra meat in the yellow paste today, likely a not-so-subtle challenge to her vegetarian nemesis, a nemesis she's encouraging me to make peace with.

The brunette in the front row complains loudly about Goth girl's smelly food. They'll have to find new people to complain about when we leave.

If we leave. I dial phone number after phone number

after phone number, certain this will be the day my hard work pays off.

Michael stomps into the room, slapping his Birkenstocks against the floor. I raise my head, our gazes meet, and he nods at me. I nod back, a habit I should really break, though it did lead to my encounters with Blaine.

Michael pauses on the threshold to his office and I hold my breath. His shoulders slump and he enters his office, shutting the door behind him.

"I think we should start our own software company," Goth girl muses.

"What?" I frown, surprised, her suggestion coming out of the blue. "I don't know anything about software *or* starting a company."

"Yes." She waves her white plastic fork. "But you know someone who does, and you can take on the administrative roles while I handle the technical stuff. I have a program I'm playing with that might revolutionize the mobile game . . . or it could fail miserably." Goth girl shrugs. "But what do we have to lose, moth?" She tilts her head. "Nothing."

We don't have anything to lose but I'm also determined to be independent. This requires money, and new companies don't pay very well. "I'll think about it." I move down the donor list. Landing a meet and greet will save my job.

"Where is she?" a woman screeches.

I recognize her high-pitched tone. I tap the receiver against my forehead as I struggle to match the voice with a face.

"I trusted her with my home, with my valued possessions." The voice grows louder.

Oh lord. Suzanna Leigh, the woman I'm house-sitting for, has returned early from Europe. My palms moisten. And she's looking for me. I scramble out of my seat. Something must have happened to the house. I take a step forward, my legs shaking.

The beautiful blonde sweeps into the room, clad in a stylish black sleeveless dress, the sweetheart neckline showing off her gravity-defying breasts. Oversized sunglasses are perched on her head.

"You—You—You—" she sputters, pointing a perfectly manicured finger at me, her blue eyes glittering.

"What is it?" I run my palms over my brown skirt. "Was there a fire?"

"A fire?" Mrs. Leigh scoffs, throwing her head back, her blond curls bouncing around her shoulders. "All of my precious art is gone. Gone." She places her hands over her chest, the gesture dramatic. "I offered you a place to stay out of the goodness of my heart, out of my sense of charity." She raises her voice as our audience grows, employees and managers gathering around us. "And this is how you repay me, by stealing from me."

"I didn't steal from you." But someone else stole from her. Mrs. Leigh gave me the task of keeping her house safe and I failed her. "Everything was there this morning." I pause. Is this true? I didn't enter every room. "I think. I noticed nothing missing." My guilt increases with each heartbeat. "I wasn't home last night," I admit.

Michael exits his office, his expression genuinely concerned.

"Anna wouldn't steal anything." Goth girl is the first person to come to my defense, standing beside me, her legs braced apart, her suit-clad shoulders shaking.

"That's likely what her father said too," Mrs. Leigh sneers, her face twisting into an ugly mask. "Before he went to prison for theft."

The room grows silent and everyone looks at me, waiting, watching for my reaction.

Mrs. Leigh knows about my father. I stare at her, cold waves of comprehension washing over me. She must have always known about him. I was set up. I didn't own anything and I thought she couldn't hurt me but I was a fool. She can take away my reputation and my freedom. "I'm not my father."

Gasps echo around me. Michael shifts his weight from his right foot to his left foot, the movement drawing my gaze. Accusations reflect in his eyes, his chin square and his stance unforgiving. I've been judged and found guilty.

"Moth's got history," Goth girl mutters. I don't look at her, unable to see the disgust on her face also.

I may not have any allies in this building but I'm not completely alone, not anymore. "I have to make a call." I rush back to my seat, search through my tote, find my phone and press redial. It rings twice.

"Anna," Blaine barks. Men are talking in the background. "What's wrong?"

"Everything. Blaine, I—"

"Put the phone down, ma'am." A policeman stands before me, his face deadly serious, one of his massive hands hovering over his gun. His partner, equally tall and broad and grim, stands by the wall. Their uniforms are crisp, light reflecting off their badges. "You're under arrest."

"Don't shoot me." I disconnect the call and drop the phone. It clatters to the metal tabletop. "I'm not resisting arrest."

Light-headed, I hold up my empty hands. This has to be a bad dream. I've never done anything wrong. I can't be getting arrested.

"Blaine," Mrs. Leigh repeats, her face paling. "How do you know Gabriel Blaine?"

"How doesn't she know Gabriel Blaine?" Goth girl grins.

My phone rings and rings and rings. It's Blaine. He's the only one who has my phone number. I can't answer it. The officer pulls my arms behind my back and restrains me, the handcuffs cool against my skin.

"This isn't real," I murmur. My legs shake, my knees threatening to buckle under me.

"Don't say another word, moth." Goth girl shushes me. "You want your lawyer. Tell him that."

"I want my lawyer," I repeat, dazed.

The officer grunts. He pats me down quickly, his fingers skimming over my breasts and between my thighs, searching places only Blaine has touched.

My coworkers watch, a mixture of horror, fascination, and disgust reflecting in their expressions. Michael does nothing, says nothing, acting as though he has never known me, has never kissed me.

"Anytime they ask you a question, you repeat that phrase." Goth girl nods. "I'll talk to your Mr. Blaine. He'll want his best legal team on this. Being framed for theft isn't a trivial thing."

Being framed. I meet Goth girl's gaze. She believes me.

"Mr. Blaine's best legal team." Mrs. Leigh sways. "This can't be. I looked into her background. She's no one. She knows no one."

The officer pushes on my shoulder and I walk, holding my head high, clinging to my pride, to the knowledge that someone believes me. My coworkers talk, not bothering to hide their snickers and sneers.

"Mr. Blaine is going to be pissed." Goth girl joins me on my walk of shame, her attitude surprisingly cheerful. "I've heard stories about what he does to people who dare to mess with his employees. All legal, of course," she adds, glancing at the arresting officer. He grunts. "Or mostly legal." Goth girl grins. "And you're more than an employee, moth."

"Officers, there's been a mistake." Mrs. Leigh chases after us, her big chest heaving and her face flushed. "I've made a mistake," she admits. "Don't arrest her. I'm dropping the charges."

Goth girl nudges me in the stomach with one of her pointy elbows and her grin spreads. The officers exchange heated looks, communicating without a word.

"I suggest you discuss this with your friend, the chief

of police, ma'am," the more verbal officer replies, clearly losing the silent argument. "Our instructions are clear. We're to arrest Miss Sampson."

I'm going to jail. The tension in my body increases with each step. My father died in jail. Bile burns the back of my throat. I'm not ready to die.

The receptionist stares at us as we enter the lobby. Her fingers fly over her phone's tiny keys. Within minutes everyone who is anyone in L.A. will know about my arrest. Even if I'm released immediately, the damage has already been done. They'll never forget. I'll always be labeled as a thief.

I take a deep breath, count to five, and exhale. I can't do this to Blaine. My arrest will scuttle his deal with Volkov, a deal he wants, a deal he's been working so hard to settle. "Don't contact Mr. Blaine, Camille."

"What? Why?" Goth girl raises her eyebrows. "You need him."

"He doesn't need me." I meet her gaze. "Promise me you won't contact him."

She holds my gaze for two heartbeats. "Okay." Goth girl sighs. "I won't contact him, but I think you're being a fool. He's Gabriel Blaine. When he finds out—and he *will* find out—he'll be even more pissed off. Heads will roll."

Mrs. Leigh wails.

Goth girl is right. When Blaine finds out about my arrest, he'll come for me. Nothing and no one will be able to stop him, not even me. Because of the pending deal with Volkov, for Blaine's sake and the sake of his employees, I hope he doesn't find out.

We exit the building. The sun is shining, rays glinting off the roof of the black and white squad car. This is real, too real. One of the police officers opens the back door. I duck my head and climb in. The interior smells sterile, like bleach. There aren't any door handles. A partition divides the front and back seats.

I'm trapped. Even if my hands were free, I couldn't escape.

The officers slide into the front seat, the gruff officer sitting behind the wheel. He doesn't start the car. They sit there. The radio cackles.

I wiggle, growing more concerned by the moment. They're two big male officers. I'm small and female and restrained.

The gruff officer turns his head, his dark eyes flash, and he grunts. The second officer glances at me, offering a small smile. He has a clipboard and a pen in his hands. "The holding cells aren't very comfortable, our booking officers are overworked, and our shift ends in five minutes."

He thinks I'll be freed, but without Blaine's help, I won't be. I slump in the seat. I'll go to jail. I won't last a week in the big house. I'm small and I don't know how to defend myself. If I had known this was my future, I would have learned karate or judo or some other type of martial arts.

If I had known, I wouldn't have agreed to house-sit for the Leighs. But then I wouldn't have met Blaine. "I love Blaine."

The officers look at me. They don't say anything.

I stare out the window at the strip of grass in front of the building. Will I ever walk barefoot in the grass again? Will I ever see the stars, hold Blaine's callused fingers, smell his horrible cigar smoke?

My soul aches and I've never felt as alone as I do right now. I can't bear the silence, the waiting.

"I know Camille said not to talk to you but I have to talk to someone, and what difference will it make if I do? The Leighs have unlimited money for legal fees and I'm broke. I don't even have my tote or my phone." I sigh. "I should have taken today off, shared my last day of freedom with Blaine."

I laugh semihysterically.

"I should have done a lot of things. I've spent my life being good, trying to fit in, to be normal, not wanting to end up like my father, and here I am, arrested for a theft I didn't do." I rest my forehead against the window, the glass cool. "Did you see the things she says I've stolen? They're glass cones. What would I do with glass cones?"

The gruff officer behind the wheel says something I can't hear. The chatty cop laughs and rolls his eyes.

I can't hear them and I doubt they can hear me. "Exactly." I relax, risking nothing by talking. "I love Blaine too much to mix him up in my drama. Can you imagine the chaos if the media gets ahold of this?"

After exchanging a glance with his partner, the serious cop starts the car and drives slowly, rolling the vehicle out of the driveway. We pass private residences, trendy pubs and boutiques.

Other people are working or shopping or eating fried

foods and drinking ice teas. I'm being transferred to jail. I'll be appointed some tired, overworked public defender while the Leighs will have a dedicated team of the best lawyers money can buy.

"What are the odds the house is broken into the same day Mrs. Leigh unexpectedly returns home?" I worry my bottom lip with my teeth, knowing in my heart I've been set up, not knowing how to prove it. "She'll have to sell those glass cones, won't she? Or do rich people insure their art?"

We drive and drive and drive through Beverly Hills, navigating the hills where the largest, most exclusive homes are located and crisscrossing the flats. I talk through my situation as the police officers sit silently in the front seat. I can't think of a solution, a way to avoid going to jail, possibly forever.

Resigned to my fate, I stare out the window at the big empty homes. My shoulders ache, my hands restrained in an unnatural position, and my stomach rumbles.

The radio crackles and the gruff officer spins the steering wheel, the tires squealing as the car is turned around. I slide along the seat and slam against the door. Our speed accelerates.

We park in front of the police station. I tilt my head back and look up at the building, dread settling low in my stomach. Is this what my father felt when he was arrested? Alone and afraid, a small player in a cruel uncaring system?

The easygoing cop opens the door, his eyes kind and understanding. His partner helps me to exit, his grip on my arms tight, as though he thinks I'll make a run for it. Where would I go? I glance around me.

A long black limousine waits in front of the building. Ted, Blaine's driver, leans on the vehicle, his arms crossed. He grins at me and some of my dread dissipates. I'm not alone. "Blaine is here," I tell the officers. He won't allow anything bad to happen to me.

The two officers look at each other and the grip on my arms loosens. "We were doing our jobs, ma'am. This isn't personal."

"Of course it isn't personal." I frown, not blaming them for my problems. "And you're doing a fine job."

We walk through the doors. Men and women in dark suits stand at the end of a long hallway. The only person I see is Blaine. He's clad in his black suit, his white shirt, and his happy yellow tie. His black hair is mussed, the rebellious lock falling across his forehead. His face is too angular to ever be called handsome.

I've never loved anyone as much as I love him, my heart bursting with emotion. "Blaine."

He turns his head and his brilliant green eyes widen. "Anna." He rushes toward me, moving faster than I've ever seen anyone move, people scattering before him.

Blaine sweeps me into his arms. His lips capture mine and I open to him, needing him inside me. He tastes of black coffee and love. He smells of sandalwood, musk, and man. He's warm and mine, and if my arms were free I'd wrap them around him and never let him go.

"Camille wasn't supposed to contact you." I gaze up at him, memorizing every line on his face, in case I never see him again. "If Volkov finds out about you associating with a thief, he won't trust you."

"You're not a thief, nymph." Blaine leans his forehead against mine, our noses touching. "And your sarcastic friend didn't contact me. I called your phone and she answered."

"I should have known she had a plan." I rub my nose against Blaine's, savoring the contact. "She agreed a bit too quickly not to contact you." I wiggle my shoulders.

He runs his hands along my arms. "What's this?" Blaine prods my handcuffs with his fingertips and frowns fiercely at the officers. "You restrained her?" he thunders, his face darkening.

"They had to put the handcuffs on me." I summon a smile, trying to ease his outrage. "The police officers were doing their jobs." Other people join us. A large heavyset man in a dark suit pushes to the forefront of the crowd, followed closely by Yen, Blaine's legal counsel. Henley stands to the side, his midnight gaze fixed on me. "The policemen were very professional and kind. I feel safer knowing they're protecting us."

"Thank you, ma'am." The gruff officer's face reddens. His partner grins. He has a dimple in his right cheek.

"Don't just stand there, officers," the heavyset man barks, his thick mane of gray hair framing a regal face. "Release Miss Sampson at once. This has all been an unfortunate misunderstanding."

"Has this been a misunderstanding?" I look to Blaine for the answer, not trusting anyone other than him.

"Yes," Blaine confirms. "Why is she still restrained?" he fumes.

The arresting officer removes my handcuffs, muttering under his breath.

"I'm free?" I shake my arms, half expecting the officer to change his mind. "Did they find the thief who broke into the Leighs' house?"

"No one broke into the Leighs' house." Blaine takes my hands and raises them closer to his face, examining my wrists thoroughly. "Suzanna remembered she'd sent her art to be catalogued." He rubs the pink marks on my pale skin.

I narrow my eyes, his explanation not making any sense. "But—"

"No buts." Blaine presses his lips to my skin, his mouth warm. "She won't be bothering us again." He flicks his tongue over my right wrist and I tremble, relishing his touch. "I always watch you, Anna." His green eyes glint.

Chapter Seven

"MEDIA IS ON their way, Mr. Blaine." Yen waves her phone. "Unless you want to be part of that circus, the two of you should leave now."

"We're leaving." Blaine wraps one of his arms around my waist. "Chief." He shakes the heavyset man's hand. "Officers." The officers stand straighter. "Thank you for taking care of my fiancée."

"Your fiancée?" I whisper as we walk outside.

"You're mine, nymph." Blaine squeezes my hip. "Forever. I want everyone to know that."

Ted opens the back door of the limousine and I climb in. Blaine follows, sitting beside me, and the door closes, the lights in the vehicle dimming.

Blaine wants to marry me, to link his name permanently with mine, with my father's deeds, with my past and with my newly acquired reputation. This will hurt Blaine. "The charges might have been dropped but society won't ever forget my arrest," I warn him. "I'll always be known as a thief."

"I'll always be known as an ex-con." Blaine slides me onto his lap, his body hard and enticingly warm. "Some doors are closed to me. Now, they'll be closed to both of us." He brushes back my hair. "Does that bother you?" He searches my face.

"Why would I want to go somewhere you're not welcome?" I frown. "I suspect I'm also unemployed."

"And how do you feel about that?" Blaine rubs his palms along my outer thighs, his touch distracting me.

I edge closer to him. "Since I'm homeless, I feel scared," I confess. "I need the money." He opens his mouth and I press my finger against his lips, stopping his offer. "Don't. I pay my own way."

Blaine nips at my finger and I pull my hand away. "Pay me whatever you want, whenever you want, that is your decision, but you're living with me. This is non-negotiable." His stern voice makes my nipples tighten. "And while you're deciding upon your next career step, you can work for me. Fran has been talking about taking a vacation for years. She didn't trust anyone previously to take her place but she does trust you."

Fran trusts me. Warmth spreads over my chest. "I don't know anything about being an assistant," I caution, not wanting to disappoint them.

"She'll train you . . . starting now." Blaine sighs. "We're returning to the office, nymph." He explores the dimples in my knees with his fingers. "I've given our ethically challenged neighbor until eight this evening to leave." His lips flatten. "And seeing her reminds me how I failed you."

"You didn't fail me." I frame his stark face between my hands. "You didn't abandon me. You came as I suspected you would when you found out about my predicament and you protected me." I press my lips against his, thanking him with all of me.

Blaine pushes back, sliding his tongue between the seam of my lips, and I allow him in, sighing my surrender, not strong enough to push him away, to do the right thing. Our tongues tumble and twist, dancing to the beat of our hearts, and his fingers tangle in my hair, pinpricks of awareness shooting over my scalp.

I straddle Blaine, hiking my skirt up, and I undulate, shamelessly rubbing against the hard ridge in his black dress pants, the proof of his desire unmistakable. I want him. I need him. I love him.

Blaine kneads my ass, my cotton panties sliding over my skin as he squeezes and releases me. I reach for his zipper, wanting him inside me.

"Not here." He catches my wrists, his fingers pressing into my skin. "Not now." Blaine brushes his cheek over mine, his breath blowing hot on my earlobe. I tremble, fluttering in his arms, as fragile as a small brown moth, trusting him to keep me safe.

"When you disconnected that call, I thought I'd lost you." Blaine shudders, his shoulders shaking. "I wasn't myself." He releases my wrists and buries his chin in the curve where my neck meets my shoulder.

I hold him, stroking his blazer-clad back with my fingers. "You must have been worried," I murmur.

"Worried?" He raises his head and our gazes meet, his eyes brilliant and hard. "I howled like a wild thing." He rakes his hands through his hair, freeing the rebellious black strands. "I wanted to kill something, someone."

I gaze at him, my mouth falling slightly open, having never had anyone care for me this much. "I love you," I blurt. My face heats.

Blaine stills. "What did you say?" His voice is dangerously quiet.

Did I mess up? Is it too early, too much, too needy, too desperate? "Ummm . . ." I stare down at his happy yellow tie, the knot tight, the silk flawless, beautiful in its simplicity.

Blaine cups my chin, raising my gaze. His eyes have darkened, their turbulence reflecting my inner turmoil. "Tell me, Anna." His tone doesn't allow any disobedience and I can't lie, not to Blaine, never to Blaine.

"I love you." My cheeks feel like they're on fire.

"Anna." Blaine crushes me to him, sealing his lips over mine, demanding, possessing, owning. I cling to his shoulders as he ravishes my mouth, whipping me with his tongue, this impossible, harsh, wonderful man punishing me for loving him.

Blaine tosses me into the far seat. I gasp as my ass slaps against the leather. He surges after me, pulling my panties off with one hard yank, leaving me bare, open to him.

His zipper rasps and, with a single driving thrust, he's inside me, his cock filling me. I scream and arch, tilting my hips to take more of him. He sinks deeper, his base pressing against my pussy lips.

"Tell me again." Blaine withdraws to his cock head and drives back into my pussy, his balls smacking against my ass. "Tell me, Anna," he orders, moving in and out of me with a breathtaking savagery.

"Love you," I pant, wrapping my legs around his waist. "Love." I suck in my breath as my ass slams against the leather seat, my skin stinging, heating. "You." I repeat my declaration over and over as he rides me, spiraling my passion upward.

I'm alive and gloriously free, free to love Blaine, to thread my fingers through his black hair, over his broad shoulders, his muscles rippling under the fabric. He growls in my ear and tugs my tank top over my head, my hair snapping with static. Cool air sweeps over my chest.

I push his jacket off his shoulders, yearning to feel his skin against mine. Blaine removes his tie and rips at his shirt. Buttons pop, the plastic circles bouncing against my stomach, and his chest is bared to me. I splay my fingers over his pectoral muscles, claiming his tanned body, his scars rough ridges under my fingertips.

He grunts, pulling me down into his thrusts, his ass cheeks clenching under my heels. My pussy hums from his powerful drives, my body coiling around his shaft.

"Not . . . deep . . . enough." Blaine flips me over, pulls me to my feet, bends me over, sticking my ass in the air. I grip the back of the seat, facing the partition dividing us from Ted, Blaine's driver.

The barrier is lowered. I meet the man's gaze in the

rearview mirror and I quiver with excitement. He's watching us fuck, watching as Blaine fills my pussy, slapping his thighs against my ass, the impact bouncing my small breasts, rattling the keys hanging on the black ribbon.

I pull my bra down, revealing everything to the driver, my pale curves and my pink nipples. Blaine grasps my hips, pressing his fingertips into my skin, marking me, as he pounds his cock into my pussy, his legs braced apart, his stance dominant.

The position is primitive, my smaller form bent under his, and he takes me like a man possessed, abandoning his renowned control to make my body his. I push back on him, thrilled by his unabashed need, his raw emotion.

"Tell me, Anna," he demands, his voice low and deep.

He needs to hear the words and I need to say them, to tell the world who owns my heart, who has earned my trust, now and forever.

"I love you." I writhe and Blaine hooks one of his arms around me, subduing me easily. "Blaine." He spears his fingers through my brown private curls.

"Love you," I squeak my capitulation. Blaine finds my clit and rubs, the circular motion winding my arousal around me tighter and tighter.

"Who do you love, nymph?" His chest slides along my back, his skin covered with a sheen of perspiration, his musk heady and male. My thighs burn and my pussy throbs, my inner walls narrowing, squeezing his shaft.

"I love you." I pant, my lungs aching, my nipples brushing against the leather seat. He sucks on my shoulder, his mouth hot, the suction exquisite, timed to match his body-shaking thrusts. "I love you, Blaine."

"Yes." His muscles mold to my curves as we strive, struggle, fight for our satisfaction. I'm close, so very close, tremors sweeping over my form. "Yes." He grazes his teeth over my skin and I whimper, dangling on the edge. "Come for me, Anna." His thumb and index finger close on my clit. "Come now." He pinches my sensitive flesh.

"Blaine," I scream and push backward. I can't move. I'm caged by Blaine's hard physique. There's no escaping him, no escaping my soul-shredding orgasm.

He drives forward mercilessly, not allowing me to catch my breath, filling me with his shaft and covering my body with his. "Anna," Blaine roars. Hot cum bathes my battered pussy, pushing me past the point of no return.

I scream and thrash under Blaine, twisting in his arms, battling to be freed yet not wanting him to ever let me go. I smoke. I smolder. I burn, my breasts, ass, pussy ablaze with heat, my world spinning in a dazzling display of brilliant flames and stunning colors. It's too much, too good, too real.

Blaine's hips jerk against me and he falls forward, flattening me. He's solid and unmoving, lying like a dead thing on top of me.

"Blaine." The leather seat muffles my voice.

He drives himself backward, taking me with him. I land on his naked lap, my legs spread, my pink pussy lips glistening with his cum. I glance at the partition. The driver has seen all of me now. I don't bother to close my thighs or cover my bare breasts.

"You're so beautiful." Blaine nuzzles his chin into my mussed hair. "And you're mine, mine to watch forever."

I swing my legs to the right, perching precariously on his thighs, trusting him to catch me should I fall. "What happened to not here and not now?"

Blaine captures my face between his rough hands. "That was before you said you loved me." He rubs one of his thumbs over my kiss-swollen bottom lip. "I love you too, nymph, more than words can express."

He loves me. I smile at Blaine, my heart filled to bursting. "But the words are still nice to hear, aren't they?"

I'm gifted with one of Blaine's rare smiles. "Yes, they're still nice to hear."

Epilogue

I STAND AT the edge of our backyard pool, watching as a small brown moth flutters on the night air, flying toward the lights. Other moths already dance around the artificial flame, a plastic barrier safeguarding them from harm. My little moth is no longer alone. She has a family or friends. She belongs.

I pull my sundress over my head and drop the garment on the stone. My frizz free hair cascades down my bare back and my nipples tighten. The clear blue water of our backyard pool ripples, its coolness calling to me, tempting me.

I rub my hands over my gently rounding stomach, beads of perspiration forming on my skin. On this scorching hot night I am the goddess of fertility, honoring all of creation. I stretch my arms upward, reaching for the moon hanging low over my head. The stars sparkle. Water rushes down rock.

"Show us, nymph."

I turn, facing my audience, allowing them to see all of me—my no longer flat stomach, my sensitive breasts, the triangle of closely cropped curls between my thighs. Two gold keys dangle from the black ribbon encircling my neck, the gold catching the light.

"Beautiful." Blaine's brilliant green eyes gleam. He sits in the lounge chair, dressed in his usual black suit and white shirt, paired with a pink tie, the color honoring our unborn baby. An unlit cigar rests in the terra-cotta ashtray. It has been there since he heard the news, Blaine refusing to smoke around me.

Behind him other men watch us, their faces and bodies shrouded by darkness. Blaine trusts them and I trust Blaine, the gold bands on our ring fingers symbolizing our unfading love. The men are his gift to both of us, their presence exciting me.

Blaine excites me. My pussy is as wet as the pool, my breasts aching for his touch. I cup my curves, offering them to him, and his lips curl upward, appreciation shining in his eyes. With him, I feel beautiful, confident in my sexual appeal.

"Sit down, Anna." Blaine pulls a patio chair closer, positioning it to face him, to face our audience. The chair's back reclines slightly, the seat cushion is thick and the armrests are padded.

I lower myself into the chair. My knees brush against Blaine's pant-covered legs and I tremble, the contact heightening my awareness of him, the cushion cool against my bare ass.

The natural ground cover rustles around us, members of our audience repositioning themselves, seeking a better view. The scent of fresh herbs mixes with sandalwood and musk, Blaine's distinctive cologne.

I pinch my nipples, the pain sharp and stimulating. Blaine's gaze lowers, tracking my movements, his eyes darkening and his dress pants tenting around his erection.

He wants me as badly as I want him. I play with my breasts, teasing and taunting him, moonlight reflecting off the gold keys. "You're overdressed." My voice is husky.

"Tonight is all about you." He reaches out and curls a tendril of my hair around his index finger. "Put your legs over the armrests."

I obey his command, opening myself completely to him, to the mysterious men watching me. Blaine peruses me leisurely, thoroughly, sweeping his gaze over my bent legs, my pale inner thighs, my glistening pink pussy. I rest my palms on my knees, allowing him to look, to see all of me.

"I've dreamed of you this way." His angular face softens. "Our child growing inside you and your naked body flush with desire. You're perfect." I feel perfect, womanly and powerful. "Show me how you touch yourself."

He knows how to touch me. I strum my feminine folds up and down, spreading my wetness, eagerly playing this sex game with him. I'm the hesitant virgin once again and he's my naughty secret, the billionaire I strip for.

I stroke my pussy with my fingers and rub my clit with my thumbs, the combination escalating my passion.

As Blaine watches me, he loosens his tightly knotted tie and undoes the top button of his dress shirt.

"You're so wet, so responsive." His eyes glow with approval. He leans forward, his head between my legs, his hot breath wafting on my inner thighs. "How do you taste?"

"I don't know." I dip into my entrance, burying my right index finger up to the joint, and I swirl, caressing my inner walls, drawing more moisture from my core. My desire spirals higher with each twist of my wrist.

I extract my finger and hold it up to him, my pussy juices glistening on my pale skin. "Taste me."

Blaine seals his lips around my finger and sucks, his cheeks indenting. His eyes roll upward, his expression blissful, a small smile curling his lips. My body pulses to the tug and pull of his mouth.

"Delicious." He releases me, my finger licked clean.

I drive into my pussy with one finger, then two, then three, stretching myself to the point of pain. Blaine's head lowers even more, moonlight streaming down on his black hair, his lips a breath away from my sensitive flesh.

I rise into each thrust of my fingers, grinding my clit into the heel of my hand. A band of passion constricts around my chest and I pant, unable to inhale enough oxygen.

I work myself with a harshness only I can, knowing my own limits. One of the men watching us groans, the quiet sound thrilling me. In my fantasy, he unfastens his pants, the dark fabric pooling around his ankles, and he strokes himself as he watches, his cock big and hard, a dab of pre-cum on his tip.

Blaine is also hard, my husband wanting me, watching me. I pump my pussy and rub my clit, pump and rub, pump and rub. My thighs quiver, my arousal building, my control fraying.

Henley is likely standing in the darkness, the big man one of our most frequent watchers. I imagine his scarred hands wrapped around his cock, his gaze fixed on my breasts, his expression heart-wrenchingly serious.

Tremors roll over me, their intensity increasing until they shake my entire body, pushing me to the sweet edge of release. I grit my teeth. I can't hold on. I can't.

"Blaine?" I ask for his permission.

He lifts his gaze and meets mine, his tanned cheeks speckled with my pussy juices. "Come for me, Anna," he orders, and I whimper with relief. "Come now."

I slam my hand against my clit. The pain breaks me and I scream, bucking upward, smacking Blaine's face with my pussy, past shame, past everything. He cups my ass, holding me, not allowing me to fall alone into the abyss.

I twist in his embrace, tethered to the world by his hands. The waves of bliss lessen and gradually fade. "I love you, Blaine," I murmur, my limbs limp and my form liquid.

"I love you, nymph." Blaine gathers me in his arms and leans back on his lounge chair, nestling my naked form into his fully clothed body. "And I love you too, baby." He kisses his palm and places his hand on my stomach.

My heart melts. I didn't think I could love Blaine more than I did mere moments ago but I do. He sees me. He loves me. He's giving me the family I've been searching for, and I know he'll always watch over us.

About the Author

CYNTHIA SAX lives in a world filled with magic and romance. Although her heroes may not always say "I love you," they will do anything for the women they adore. They live passionately. They play hard. They love the same women forever.

Cynthia has loved the same wonderful man forever. Her supportive hubby offers himself up to the joys and pains of research, while they travel the world together, meeting fascinating people and finding inspiration in exotic places such as Istanbul, Bali, and Chicago.

Please visit her on the web at www.CynthiaSax.com.

Visit www.AuthorTracker.com for exclusive information on your favorite HarperCollins authors.